What the critics are saying…

"This is the first book I have ever read by Ms. Wine, but it will not be the last. She is a talented author with a knack for creating suspenseful scenes that left me on the edge of my seat. Dream Surrender is a fantastic book that I am sure I will reread often." ~ *Susan White Reviewer for Karen Find Out About New Books Reviewer for Coffee Time Romance*

Five Angels "What a fascinatingly scary idea. What if a kiss endangered your life? How would you react? Ms. Wine does a fabulous job bringing this senario to life." ~ *Serena Fallen Angel Reviews*

Dream Surrender

Mary Wine

ELLORA'S CAVE
ROMANTICA PUBLISHING

An Ellora's Cave Romantica Publication

www.ellorascave.com

Dream Surrender

ISBN # 1419952463
ALL RIGHTS RESERVED.
Dream Surrender Copyright© 2005 Mary Wine
Edited by: Sue-Ellen Gower
Cover art by: Syneca

Electronic book Publication: March, 2005
Trade paperback Publication: September, 2005

Excerpt from *Dream Shadow* Copyright © Mary Wine, 2004

Warning:

The following material contains graphic sexual content meant for mature readers. *Dream Surrender* has been rated *S-ensuou*s by a minimum of three independent reviewers.

Ellora's Cave Publishing offers three levels of Romantica™ reading entertainment: S (S-ensuous), E (E-rotic), and X (X-treme).

S-*ensuous* love scenes are explicit and leave nothing to the imagination.

E-*rotic* love scenes are explicit, leave nothing to the imagination, and are high in volume per the overall word count. In addition, some E-rated titles might contain fantasy material that some readers find objectionable, such as bondage, submission, same sex encounters, forced seductions, etc. E-rated titles are the most graphic titles we carry; it is common, for instance, for an author to use words such as "fucking", "cock", "pussy", etc., within their work of literature.

X-*treme* titles differ from E-rated titles only in plot premise and storyline execution. Unlike E-rated titles, stories designated with the letter X tend to contain controversial subject matter not for the faint of heart.

Also by Mary Wine:

A Wish, A Kiss, A Dream anthology

Beyond Boundaries

Dream Shadow

Dream Specter

Ellora's Cavemen: Tales from the Temple III anthology

Alcandian Quest

Tortoise Tango

Beyond Lust

Dream Surrender

Dream

Trademarks Acknowledgement

The author acknowledges the trademarked status and trademark owners of the following wordmarks mentioned in this work of fiction:

Hummer: Hummer: AM General Corporation
Jell-O: Kraft Foods Holdings, Inc.

Chapter One

It just wasn't fair.

Not a bit. Everyone else had sighed over the bride, delighted in the scent of fresh flowers and felt deep, moving emotion as the minister issued the words that joined the couple in wedlock.

Contemplating the shoreline, Loren tried to remind herself that she always felt depressed at weddings. So why did she let herself get roped into attending this one?

Why didn't particularly matter at the moment. Stepping off the porch she moved onto the beach. Her shoes sank into the sand, and reaching down, she pulled them off her feet. Tucking the shoes under the railing, Loren set off again, smiling as her bare toes sank into the tiny grains beneath her.

The night wasn't a total loss—Amanda sure did know how to pick a spot. The reception was being held with a half-mile stretch of private beach for a backdrop. Music spilled out the open doors of the banquet hall, but as she put more distance between herself and the party, the sounds of the surf took dominance.

It was nothing but a self-centered indulgence, but Loren was in the mood to answer temptation's call. The night was perfect, the breeze lazy, and no one else was in sight!

Perfection.

But time was not on her side tonight. Turning around, Loren set herself back toward her social responsibilities. Another round of small talk and she could escape before the guests' blood alcohol levels rose too high.

She made it just two steps before she saw him. Maybe it really shouldn't have surprised her to find another person on the beach. There was just something surreal about her companion. Nothing but moonlight spilled over him but her eyes picked out his features.

He stood surveying the surf, his body seemingly at ease. Sensation crept up her spine as she noted the sheer size of him. His arms, like his chest, were coated with thick muscle. Even the denim of his jeans betrayed the fact that his legs held the same level of fitness.

It wasn't just his size that captured her attention. There was something not quite tame about him. The way he stood looking out to sea didn't betray that fact—it was an increasing urge she felt to seek shelter. Loren shook her head to dispel her foolishness. If half a glass of champagne was going to her head this much, it was past her bedtime.

Maybe tapping into her emotions was unethical, but at the moment Rourke really didn't care. He was sick of the protocol. Everyone seemed to have an idea on just when and how his psychic sense should be used. What they all missed was the fact that it was a part of him. Sometimes a man's discipline just couldn't hold back his nature.

It was her fault anyway. The way she moved was far too erotic. It wasn't so much the dress she wore, but the way her body moved beneath the fabric. There was a twist and sway to her hips that begged for closer inspection.

Reaching out further, Rourke tapped into her emotions. A smile lifted the corners of his mouth. She was watching him, running her eyes over his body as she considered the desire that was rising up inside her own.

Turning his head, he caught her eyes. Hers widened slightly in surprise, but she brought her emotions under control before he caught the physical signs that her body could give him. But he felt them anyway. Caution was coursing along her nerves as she noticed his interest. The battle she was waging for control, Rourke intended her to lose. Once she discarded the mantle of respectability that her morals were demanding, they could share what promised to be a searing passion.

Loren was never touching another glass of champagne as long as she lived!

She was practically drooling over the man. With her luck tonight, he probably could see it written across her face. Grinding her teeth together, Loren tried to pull herself together enough to walk back to the reception.

The way he stood there watching her made the idea of crossing his path disturbing. Moving her eyes over his form, she marveled at the strength of the man. It floated on the air. It wasn't just his body, it seemed to be deeply rooted inside his being. Her skin was sensitive to the magnetic pull. Her entire body was pulsing with a need that Loren had spent years banishing.

Fascination replaced her misgivings as Loren watched the way he moved. Silently. His body moved across the shoreline with a confidence that confirmed his strength. Loren found herself watching his approach with a intensity that refused to allow her practical instincts any chance to be heard.

With fluid grace, he came closer. Tilting her head back, Loren caught a glimpse of the most startling emerald eyes just seconds before he pulled her body into his with a single movement and his mouth settled onto hers in firm ownership.

Her senses rioted as the sheer volume of impulses overwhelmed them. Too many points of contact sent their signals racing along her nerves into a brain that was struggling to sort them into logical order.

His body moved hers as it pleased, turning and surrounding her flesh as his lips engaged in an assault that demanded complete compliance. The intimate invasion forcing her to yield as his tongue sought her own. Twisting and thrusting, he took her mouth in the way that his body promised to follow. His hips thrust against her, showing her the proof of his intentions.

"Wait… We can't do this!"

"I think we can."

His voice held as much iron as his body did, the deep, determined tone settling over her ears. Her own inability to deny the truth of her mutual interest caused true fear to rise up inside her.

Loren sighed as her fingertips became ultrasensitive. Her hands traveled across the shirt-covered expanse of his chest. She ran her hands back and forth over his chest as her fingertips delighted with the hard muscle they found. Longing sprang up as she tried to force her brain to function.

"I can't do this."

Pulling his head up, Rourke considered the female in his arms. He could smell the passion on her body, feel it seeping into the pores of his skin. At the moment the sand beneath them would serve just fine. The panic in her voice was the only thing causing him to question his purpose.

Searching her thoughts, he considered what he found. If she had a boyfriend at that reception, her feelings didn't run very deep. No, her concern stemmed from the strength of her own arousal.

Lowering his mouth again, Rourke took possession of her lips. He captured the moan that escaped from her as she lost her battle to ignore their mutual attraction. Her body leapt as passion ignited inside it. Her hips twisted into his as her hands moved over him in blatant invitation.

Thoughts simply refused to form. Loren couldn't stop her hands and she didn't try. He just smelled so very male. It was intoxicating in its intensity. His body was so hard. She was craving it. Her fingers clawed at his shirt searching for the skin she could smell.

"Come with me."

He pulled her by their joined hands a full thirty feet before her mind cleared enough to offer protest. Digging her feet into the sand, she pulled him to a halt.

"Right here is fine with me."

"No!" This time the sounds from the wedding reception intruded on her reckless behavior with stinging awareness. Loren thrust her passion aside, grabbing at the control she'd somehow lost.

"I can not do this." Forcing each word out, Loren used their truth to steady her resolve.

"Whoever he is, I'd say it's time to break it off."

"It's not that simple."

"The truth is always simple. It's when you start to deceive yourself that things get complicated."

Their hands were still joined. Loren stared at his flesh as it imprisoned hers and lamented the facts that would limit her to this last taste of him. What her body demanded just could never be.

"I agree, but some things are just not meant to happen."

The longing in her eyes caused Rourke to hesitate before replying. Maybe she was afraid of breaking up with the guy.

"I won't let him hurt you."

One quick step and a simple twist broke the hold on her hand. Moving further away she turned to survey her companion. Forcing her eyes to take in the aggression in his, she coupled it with the harsh lesson that life had taught her long ago. Men always manipulated women to suit their needs. This one was no different. He'd protect her 'til he became bored, then she'd be on her own.

"I can take care of myself."

"No, honey, what you need only I can take care of."

An angry flush burned her face as Loren had to fight off the warmth spreading through her body in response to his words. Sex, even hot sex, wouldn't solve anything. It would just complicate her life.

Taking a closer look at him, her eyes noted the precise neatness to his dress. Simple jeans and a flannel shirt but the shirt was pressed to perfection while his black hair was clipped to razor shortness. The stance of his body betrayed a level of alertness rarely found in the civilian male.

Coupled with his strength, Loren identified exactly what manner of predator she'd attracted tonight. A SEAL, a Ranger or maybe even a Marine Special Operations. His eyes still glittered with the conquest he fully expected to make of her.

Well, there was always one way to deter this kind of man.

"I'm married."

* * * * *

She never remembered saying good night to her hosts. Loren had crawled out of her car and made it up the stairs to her bedroom before she felt the grip of her encounter releasing her.

Sinking onto her bed she stared at the reflection in her mirror. It had been a really long time since she'd been so incredibly stupid.

That was the last time she'd listened to her body when it came to a man. Lying back, she sent her fist into the pillow. Frustration was gnawing away at her flesh as she tried to remind herself just what listening to it would get her.

Still…she was doing better tonight than when she was sixteen. Tonight she was taking frustration to bed instead of a husband. The security of that idea let Loren slip into sleep. Yes, sexual frustration was far better than the unpredictable nature of a man.

Chapter Two

His hands were shaking so badly that Dr. Frank Rinehart couldn't make out the lab report anymore. He didn't need the computer-generated words to reinforce his rising panic. Despite the regular county-required drills, they just weren't ready to cope with a medical disaster of this magnitude. The possible number of infected victims was spinning his brain out of control.

"Doctor?"

Frank forced his eyes up to the men waiting. He shoved his hands into the pockets of his lab coat to still the increased tremor his current company inspired. Several of them were restlessly pacing the confines of the conference room. Their leader stood deathly still as he waited for his information.

"Yes...well, we cannot be certain 'til we grow a culture but... Maybe it might be best if you sat down."

Black brows slanted over a piercing green glare in response.

"No, I suppose that won't be necessary. We must begin quarantine immediately. If this is Ebola Tai Forest, the possibility for contamination is immense."

"How complete a quarantine do you suggest?"

"Anyone on your team and anyone you gentlemen might have engaged in relations with."

Rourke flashed his eyes over his men. They had been back on American soil less than twenty-four hours. Most of that time they'd spent in the air. The negative looks he received told him none of his men had found time to engage in anything as of yet. That left just him.

Damn! Why had he been so hot to get into her pants anyway? He'd been tighter before, that didn't explain why a simple walk on a beach turned into an encounter that was still wedged in the back of his mind.

"Why" didn't matter at the moment.

"Define 'relations', Doctor."

"Intercourse definitely, but any manner of exchange of bodily fluids could account for contamination."

Rourke cast his eyes over his men again. They shook their heads before they began to move restlessly about the room again. His own body was screaming with tension but control was something he'd learned to pull deeper than most. If his unit was contaminated he'd move them out immediately before the symptoms began to surface.

It was damn poor luck that Cal Worth didn't collapse until he'd made it off the base. Now Rourke faced the problem of getting his man out of a civilian hospital before any word leaked out to the public.

"Get Worth onto the bird and stand by."

"Yes, sir!"

"That man needs to stay right here. You can't remove him, it's against the law!"

Rourke's men didn't bat an eye as they carried out their orders. The door swung shut behind them as the doctor sputtered out his protests.

"This is now a classified matter, Dr. Rinehart. We have procedures to deal with this. I'm sure you can agree that it would be best to remove a possible threat of this nature from such a major metropolitan area."

"Yes. But can you be certain of a complete containment?"

The doctor posed a good question. Not knowing her name was going to prove a bit tricky. Rourke could still feel her. His mind held the link necessary for him to track her down, but if the local law enforcement decided to challenge him on removing her, then Rourke would rather not be distracted by the amount of his attention he'd need to utilize his tracking abilities.

"There is one exposed civilian."

"I can have the police pick them up immediately. With a disease this deadly I do not suggest any delay."

The doctor was already reaching for the wall-mounted telephone. Rourke frowned as he considered the complications of tracking someone through the Los Angeles area. There was just too big a population. Risking possible exposure of his psychic abilities, much less the fact that he operated with a team of Rangers, was just not advisable. The civilian population would not receive that sort of information very well.

It might be wise to try a more conventional route first. The local detectives might be able to track her down in a reasonable amount of time. The doctor's hands shook as Rourke gave him a description, and the physical reaction only reminded him of why he didn't want to deal with civilians during this quarantine. There was no point in getting nervous until they had positive proof that there was a direct threat to their lives.

"Wait a minute, I was at that wedding last night. It was one of our residents here who got married. But I don't recall just whom you are describing. There weren't many single women at the wedding."

"She claimed to be married."

The doctor flashed him a scathing look. Rourke really didn't care. The passion hiding inside that woman was hot enough for him to feel twenty feet away. Her husband was clearly a fool.

"Well, still there are only two women that fit this description. One of them is pregnant and the other I don't believe is married."

"How pregnant?"

"Advanced."

"It's not her."

Rourke smiled. So the little vixen lied to throw him off the track? Well, that could make a quarantine together rather interesting. After all, he had already contaminated her. Any repeats wouldn't change a thing.

"Maybe I should call for a guest list. This just isn't Loren's style."

"It would be quicker to have the woman brought in for identification."

"She's already here. But I'm certain it's a waste of time. Loren is very clear about her views on men."

Despite the doctor's confidence, the man began moving toward the door as he spoke. Rourke followed on the man's heels. If this Loren was his woman then he intended to close this issue immediately. The fewer eyes that set on him the better. Keeping a low profile was essential to his unit's survival. Taking a civilian with them was going to produce a huge security question. Rourke would deal with that just as soon as he found her. If the doctor could provide the information to finding her then it would prevent anyone else from becoming involved.

Reaching one of the hospital's elevators, the doctor punched the top floor before turning to face Rourke again. The man's eyes held a critical look again. Rourke sent him a piercing one back. The civilian world didn't have a clue as to the details of his life and therefore was not equipped to judge his actions. Forming any sort of permanent attachment to a woman could have deadly results for her. He rarely learned very much about his partners because a little information spilled into the wrong ears could get them killed.

"Carol, page Loren."

"She's inbound now. ETA is two minutes."

The nurse never looked up but fired off her information as she continued to wrap a paper gown about another doctor's chest. Her assistance was clearly needed as the man stood with his gloved hands held straight up into the air to prevent them from becoming contaminated.

Two other doctors stood nearby in similar positions. They faced another set of elevator doors as they waited for their incoming patient.

"You'll want to move back."

"I know what a trauma center looks like, Doctor."

"Yes, I imagine you do."

The red light above the doors flashed in warning. The waiting teams snapped to attention as they awaited their duties. The doors of the elevator opened in a violent motion as a man's body came falling across the threshold. The obvious victim of a powerful kick, the paramedic tumbled over his own body as his partner was left to the struggle their patient was intent on waging.

The close quarters of the elevator didn't allow for the waiting doctors to lend any assistance to the battle. With the body of the first paramedic sprawled in the doorway, the waiting doctors couldn't get to their patient. Struggling with the enraged patient, the second paramedic brutally flipped her charge over before using her body to pin him to the stretcher. Her partner regained his feet and pulled the entire struggle from the elevator, allowing the waiting teams to assist her.

"Are you all right, Loren?"

"That will conclude our wrestling demonstration for this evening." Investigating her shirtfront, Loren decided there weren't enough buttons left to close her uniform.

"Carol, you might want to call security. This guy's family is coming en masse."

Lord, the stupidity of some of their city residents was amazing. Shaking her head, Loren headed for her locker before her pager went off again. Responding with her bra showing just didn't appeal to her.

"So, she's not married."

Dr. Rinehart stared in fascination as Rourke's eyes glowed. There was an intent frown displayed on the man's face.

"I just don't understand it. Loren doesn't take very well to men."

"She's deadly at ten paces." The second paramedic issued his comment as he came back through the doorway, leaving his patient to the care of the trauma room staff. The curses sailing out of the treatment room indicated the lack of gratefulness the youth had for his care.

"Jim, you'll need to call in another partner. I have to quarantine Loren immediately."

"For what?"

"That's classified."

Stepping back, the paramedic stared at his face for a moment before his pager went off and he looked back at the doctor with a raised eyebrow. Loren came back into view as the pager on her belt echoed her partner's.

"I thought it was a full moon last week," she grumbled as she tried to fix her uniform top.

"Did you mean right now?"

Loren looked at her partner like he'd lost his mind. The man was looking at Dr. Rinehart as he asked his question.

"Do our pagers know any other time frame?"

Loren stared at her partner as he gave her a confused look. Snapping his pager out of his hand, she silenced the alarm the unit was issuing, wondering just how long Jim intended to stand there staring at her.

"Dr. Rinehart says you're off duty."

"Excuse me?"

Flipping her eyes about, Loren pegged the doctor with them. She didn't have time for another of the medical staff's games! Being the only female life flight paramedic was getting a little old.

Just how she'd missed seeing him, Loren didn't know. A man like that was not designed for blending in. He was standing with his arms folded over his chest and she found herself tipping her chin up to catch a good look at his face. Her stomach dropped a full three inches as she found the green eyes. The corners of his mouth twitched up in a grin as he watched her take him in. There was absolutely nothing friendly about that grin. It was pure intent.

"I believe you have…ah…met this man?"

The obvious indication caused Loren to bristle. The man in question was trouble. In big capital letters, but that didn't mean she was going to sit there and let Dr. Rinehart critique her for inappropriate behavior!

"Quarantine for what?"

"Ebola Tai Forest."

A curse slipped from Jim's mouth as he took a step away from her. Loren would have liked to step away from herself as well. Ebola Tai Forest was no laughing matter. One of the four strains of the Ebola virus, the disease held an eighty percent fatality rate. Add to that the fact that no one understood yet why twenty percent of the infected victims survived.

It wasn't something Los Angeles County saw very much of. Only a very occasional traveler was suspect. Her eyes wandered over her company again as she noted the clear proof of his military training. The details were easier to see in the lighting of the hallway. The man's body had been molded into a weapon. He was also a very likely candidate for transporting a disease like this across the globe. There was no point in asking him if he'd been in Africa, the fact that he was standing in front of her confirmed that.

And the man had kissed her very deeply and very thoroughly. Fluid exchange was the number one method of contamination.

"There are words to describe men like you."

"Nice to see you again, Loren."

Nasty, dirty little words and Loren truly felt that this man would wear them well. It was really too bad that she'd made that bet with herself about not swearing. Tonight seemed like a perfectly appropriate time for cussing.

"I take it you will not deny your…ah…relations with this man?"

Forget swearing, Loren was currently ready to begin with physical assault! Doctor Rinehart could just be grateful that she intended to break his neck in a trauma room! Jim was choking on his amusement and doing a very poor job of keeping the sounds to himself.

"You know, I need to run now."

Loren watched her partner hightail it into the elevator. Jim's mouth worked as much overtime as she did. By shift change, every firehouse in the county would be making up their own version of her love affair.

"Well then, I suppose I should leave you to this situation."

Watching the doctor begin his trip back down the hallway, Loren was left facing her green-eyed dilemma.

"Dr. Rinehart?" Loren sent her voice after the doctor as he scurried away from possible infection. The man stepped between her and Rinehart.

"I'm sorry, did we forget to mention that this is now a classified matter?"

"Just how classified?"

Whoever he was, he grinned at her question before letting his eyes inspect her. From the top of her head to the black toes of her boots, Loren didn't think he missed a single detail of her body. Returning to her face, his mouth settled into a smug expression of victory.

"Classified is classified."

"Umm-humm. Well, if that means you're planning on disappearing without so much as an introduction, have a nice life. But if you were planning on inviting me along, you can call up my captain and explain this little vacation to him. I happen to like my job. A whole lot."

"Rourke Campbell, and we'll have plenty of time to get acquainted."

"Don't bet on it."

But he was. Loren could see his eyes glowing with anticipation. The look on his face made her look closer to see if he actually began to lick his chops over her. Well, it was a bet that he would be losing! It took a little more than sex appeal to get her pants off.

"Dr. Rinehart."

Loren jumped at the command his voice issued. To date he had used a deeply sensual tone with her. The deep rumble that sounded down the hallway called up an urge to straighten her back. Frank reacted like a new marine recruit. The doctor snapped to attention, his back ramrod straight.

"I trust you can deal with the fire department discreetly. We wouldn't want a public panic."

"No, of course not."

"Thank you."

Seeing this man in her hospital had robbed Loren of her first impression of him. The second he dismissed the doctor his body executed that silent grace that she'd first noticed about him. A quick step and he'd grasped her biceps as he used the hold to propel her body toward the elevator. Her feet stumbled to keep pace but if he noticed, the information never gained a response. They were already inside the elevator before she managed a retort.

"This only goes to the landing pad on the roof."

His green eyes regarded her with amusement. The same kind a cat used when it was tormenting a mouse. Fine! If the man wanted to waste his time, then she appeared to have plenty to spare now as well.

The door opened and Loren stepped out onto the roof. She was completely at home here. Her feet traced a path that her body knew by heart. Her stride faltered as she took in the helicopter sitting on the pad. Instead of one of the county's medical units, this thing was deepest black. The sleek lines screamed out a modern edge that her civilian aircraft lacked.

"You have style, Mr. Campbell. I'll give you that."

"Major."

And pride. An officer to boot. That really didn't surprise her. The tone the man was capable of using was pure steel. Dr. Rinehart was one of the pickiest doctors in the hospital. Watching him jump when told to was almost worth having to deal with Major Campbell.

But not quite.

"This is a Panther."

The words came out of her mouth as an afterthought. Loren was too busy looking over the top-secret aircraft to pay her mouth any mind. Nicknamed the Red Eye, these helicopters were cutting edge. They were equipped with the newest laser technology and primarily deployed for searching. They also carried heavy artillery to allow them to complete their searches in friendly skies or not.

Three of his men turned deadly eyes onto their guest. Rourke watched her examine his bird with suspicion as well. No civilian should even know the name of this aircraft, much less anything about it. That suspicion was rapidly growing as he watched Loren run a critical eye over key areas of the helicopter. It would seem that she knew more about it than just the name.

"Her roommate works for NASA." Sergeant Gilmore glared at Loren as he spoke. The Ranger clearly didn't like the familiar way Loren looked at his aircraft.

Her roommate's career was over! Rourke was going to see to that personally! The woman was married, but she was a liar. Sergeant Gilmore would have stated it if the man was her husband. It would appear she also kept company with a man who didn't understand just what classified meant. That kind of sloppiness got men like Rourke killed.

His little lapse of sanity was spreading further. If Loren lived with a man it was very likely he was contaminated as well.

"Pick the guy up."

Rourke really shouldn't have been quite so disappointed but he was. Climbing aboard his aircraft, he left Loren to his junior officer. He would leave the woman to her adultery.

Oh, this was priceless. Loren found it nearly impossible to contain her amusement. Major Campbell was clearly annoyed with her. Yes sir, the man had his boxers in a twist for sure.

It was just the right sort of punishment for his ego. The man needed to be brought down a peg and Loren was happy to help. Men always thought that what was good for them was unacceptable for women. Major Campbell held no reservations about making a pass at a complete stranger, but Lord forbid she should have a boyfriend.

No, she was expected to be the pristine virgin just waiting for him to sweep her off her feet…

Ha! Not in the real world. Loren very much doubted that he was a virgin and she hated the double standard the man harbored.

The rotors of the helicopter began their rotation as Loren snapped her harness into place. She was going to enjoy this ride. The county didn't operate anything quite so modern. Feeling the power contained in the Panther made her nerves zing with anticipation of the coming flight.

And then she was going to have the pleasure of watching Major Campbell eat his hat. Loren didn't need a boyfriend. After all, it was really much more satisfying to watch the men around her make complete asses of themselves.

Rourke Campbell was off to a wonderful start.

* * * * *

"I flew up here in a Panther, Mom! A Red Eye Panther! You should see the laser targeting screens. I know the specs but when they are responding to the trigger sensors the precision is excellent!"

Her son launched into a complete technical explanation of the computer programming abilities of the helicopter that transported him. Loren forced her mind to try and understand at least half of the information being carried in her son's words.

At fourteen, Toby had already surpassed Loren in height and was well on his way to becoming a giant. Slim and reedy, her son reminded her of a colt—all legs and energy.

"You're his mother?"

"Why, yes. I'm quite certain I told you I am married. Children sometimes come along in such relationships." Loren fluttered her eyelashes a few times before returning her attention to her son. Oh yes. Rourke Campbell was entirely too much fun.

That woman needed to be hauled off to bed. Her husband sure as hell wasn't taking care of her. If she were his, Rourke would spend the rest of the night working that starch out of her tight little backside.

Damn it!

She wasn't a liar, which brought Rourke back to finding her extremely intriguing. The sight of her son forced him to acknowledge the fact that she belonged to another man. Even if the guy was foolish enough to stay away from her bed, she was still married.

That was a line that Rourke wouldn't cross.

But something was still off. There was no way a fourteen-year-old kid worked for NASA. Rourke headed for his office to discover just where his field information was wrong. While he was at it, Rourke intended to find the name of the man who was such an idiot as to abandon a woman like Loren. Maybe the guy didn't like kids. She wouldn't be the first wife to discover that flaw in her husband after the baby was born.

Ahh, who was he kidding? Rourke wanted to believe she was alone because he wanted her. The woman oozed sex appeal. His body was pulsing even now as he watched her follow her son around one of his helicopters.

She was one hell of a package. Loren wasn't slim. Instead her body was tight and full-figured. Sandy blonde hair was twisted on top of her head but the unruly strands refused to stay trapped and were catching the sunlight. A pair of light green eyes betrayed an Irish heritage. Her position with a fire department spoke volumes about her personality. This woman was a livewire. That passion had attracted him on that beach and it was even more apparent now.

Rourke shook his head as he resigned himself to disappointment. Another man had noticed her much earlier in life. Lucky bastard.

"You bitch!"

Halfway across the landing pad, Rourke turned back at a dead run. The violence expressed in those two words communicated itself down to his soul. Loren was the only female on the site. One of his men had taken major exception to her. Rourke didn't care what the reason was but the man was deadly furious and Rourke needed to intercede.

"You said it was a girl!"

"The doctor told you that. Maybe you should have waited around to make sure."

Loren issued her words with precise pronunciation. It was a scene she'd often considered having to endure but it was still a shock to come face to face with her husband.

Fourteen years wasn't long enough. Rage was boiling up inside her as red-hot as the day he'd deserted her.

Chris had always turned to violence when words escaped him. Today was no exception. Despite the years of separation, Loren clearly read the signs of her husband's exploding temper. She watched the muscles of his chest tighten as he raised his fist to speak for him.

One thing had changed in fourteen years—Loren wasn't going to stand there cringing in fear while her husband hit her. She watched his arm as it swung at her face. Her body responded with beautiful obedience to the hours of training she'd forced herself to endure.

Chris never expected her to move and she took full advantage of his ignorance. Raising her arm to block his strike, she raised a leg and executed a solid front snap kick that sent her husband flying into the dirt. Chris raised a stunned face to her as his mouth issued another round of filthy language that Loren remembered all too well.

"I am not sixteen anymore! The next time you hit me, I promise you I will make it the last!"

* * * * *

Three hours later, Loren was still staring at her husband. Major Campbell might have banished her to the front porch of his house but there was no way she was taking her eyes off of Chris!

But she really wanted to know just what Rourke had said to him. Night had fallen hours ago but her temper was keeping her plenty warm. Chris appeared to have been given first watch and stood just off to the side of the landing pad with a semiautomatic rifle slung over his shoulder.

Loren wasn't a fool. She'd kept careful track of her husband's whereabouts. It was the only logical thing to do when the man had little compunction about trying to kill her with his fists. That was one of the main reasons she'd never divorced the man. The Army had very clear rules about spouses. Being Chris' legal wife meant she was given information on just where her husband was.

"Mom, your hands are turning blue."

"Toby, I am having a really bad day."

"Yeah, I sort of noticed that."

Her son's offbeat humor was about the only thing that could slice through her anger. Loren tilted her head to the side and looked up at her son. She really was lucky to have such a great kid.

"There's dinner inside. It's worse than John's cooking."

Loren made a face in response. John Phelps was the engineer at one of her local stations. The man was determined to become a chef and he had a long way to go. But since she'd landed her job with Los Angeles County five years ago, Toby was eating at a lot of fire stations due to the twenty-four hour shifts she worked.

"All right, I will endeavor to get over myself."

Her son flashed her grin before he turned and loped into the house. Loren took a last look at Chris before she forced her body to follow. There was no point in standing there nursing her pride. She'd made the stupid mistake of marrying the man and there was nothing she could do to fix that now. Too young to know better, she'd let her young heart lead her straight into the lion's den.

"Lavender Rain?"

"Mom hates her name."

Just her luck. Having left one problem male outside, Loren now had the privilege of facing down the second one. This quarantine was going to be very long.

"Mom says it's a side effect of having grandparents who attended Woodstock." Toby picked up a dinner plate and began piling food onto it.

"You were born to a pair of flower children?"

"No, only my mother suffers from that disease."

"So just where was your father while she was signing the birth certificate?"

Loren considered ignoring Rourke's question. Unless she missed her guess, the man knew the answer already. But you couldn't prove it by the look on his face. His expression sat solid as granite and gave absolutely nothing away.

But she did have eyes in her head. Top-secret aircraft, Rangers patrolling the area—if Major Rourke Campbell didn't have the means to pulling every last bit of personal information about her then she'd eat her shoes. The man was currently conducting an honesty test.

"My dad was chasing his stripes."

"You mean he was serving his country."

The hard expression that crossed his eyes was a familiar one. Loren had seen it on her father's face too many times to count. It was a look that only men who'd shared the bitter experience of combat could wear. There was a brotherhood relayed in the emotion.

Seeing it cross Rourke's face sent a slight tingle down her spine. This man was completely untamed. He pushed his body to the limits of endurance because he relied on his conditioning to stay alive.

"Before you say it, your information is correct. Toby does work for NASA."

The woman wasn't a liar, but she was sure provocative. Rourke considered her as she picked at a plate of food. She was also very perceptive—he was still waiting to hear back from the boy's superior to confirm his employment. But Florida was on the opposite side of the continent and Rourke wouldn't get that confirmation for another four hours when the sun came up at Cape Canaveral

Moving his eyes over the boy in question, Rourke assessed him. The kid was working on his third plate. God only knew where he was putting all that food. There wasn't an ounce of spare flesh on the kid's lanky frame. Toby sent him a grin as he stuffed another forkful of chicken into his mouth. The kid should be discussing the latest video game craze not the finer points of his Panther.

The problem was the kid knew more about the aircraft than Rourke did.

"My son is a genius."

"A what?"

Loren didn't take offense as Rourke almost snarled his question. She was really quite used to disbelief in connection to her son's intelligence level. She was still trying to get used to the idea herself.

"As in, top one percent of the population on the planet."

"Ah ha."

Loren simply tossed her head. There was no reason for her to wear her tongue out trying to convince this guy of anything. Rourke Campbell would still wait until he'd gained that confirmation from NASA.

Laying her fork aside, she decided that it was a shame some poor chicken had died only to end up tasting so very similar to chalk.

Loren's acceptance of his disbelief wasn't what Rourke wanted. She was completely comfortable with letting the matter rest. No evidence laid out to sway his opinion, no heartfelt jumble aimed at polishing up her son's image.

That left him with only one conclusion. The boy was some kind of genius.

"Why aren't you at M.I.T. earning multiple doctorates?"

Toby ran an arm across his mouth before he answered the question.

"They've got a problem with a project that they think I can solve. When that's done I get to go off to college."

"Ah ha."

"Mom, I'm gonna go check the onboard computer for discrepancies in programming translation to application."

Her son was halfway out the door when Loren dragged him to a halt. Rourke didn't even suspect the kid could move that fast, but his mother was used to his abrupt changes in focus.

"Toby, these people don't quite buy the whole security clearance thing yet. Do me a favor and don't get shot. I'm off duty for a change."

"Ohh." The kid's disappointment didn't last for long. His eyes shifted for a mere second before he chose another target to aim his attention on. Another long-legged launch and he hauled his backpack from the tabletop and loped off into the family room.

"What is he up to?"

"He's looking for a power outlet to set up his system."

"And then what is he going to do?"

Loren slowly smiled. Her son was a handful. She was going to enjoy watching the major here try and keep up with him. Her smile faded as she considered just why they were both here.

"Why don't you enlighten me about this whole thing? I'd rather not have Toby overhear the details."

"You're a paramedic, what more do you need to know?"

"Let's start with how certain you are of contamination." His lips pulled back into a wide smile. "I was referring to your contamination, I remember mine."

"Good."

Dropping her plate, Loren glared at her tormentor. Propped against the kitchen counter, his lazy stance didn't fool her one bit.

"I'm a married woman, so forget it."

That got his attention. Half a second and he was standing at his full height. One step and he'd closed the distance between their bodies to mere inches. Her breath caught in her throat as she tipped her head back to get caught in his emerald stare. All playfulness was gone like it had never been. His face was etched in solid granite as he pegged her with a penetrating stare.

"I have a man down. Preliminary blood work shows exposure to the virus. Seven days will show if he's going to develop the disease." He finished closing the gap 'til his face was a split second from touching her own. His breath hit her lips as he stopped before completing the kiss. "And you need a divorce."

The screen door slapped shut behind Rourke as he left, letting Loren collapse in relief into a chair. Her entire body was shaking. It had to be impossible to be so very aware of a man. Her nerve endings were screaming and he hadn't laid a finger on her.

Seven days might as well be seven years.

Chapter Three

"Paul's been trying to reach you but your phone's not getting a clear signal. These mountains have a large iron core and it's producing a lot of static. But I've changed the setting on your dish network so you should get that signal now."

Loren's son loped back into his living room a half second after he finished talking. Rourke's phone buzzed for attention almost on cue. Staring at the empty doorway, Rourke grabbed the cellular device from his pocket.

"Campbell."

"Your tone implies that I've caught you at a bad time, Major."

"Dr. Jasper?"

"Yes, your message did say it was urgent."

"It is... Stand by." Ripping a towel off its drying rack, Rourke pulled it across his face and neck. Three hours of hard running and that woman was still stuck inside his skull! "All right, Doctor, I apologize. I need some information on a Tobias Loren."

"Toby. Yes, quite a unique young man."

"How unique?"

"You would have to meet the young man to know, Major. I became acquainted with him when he broke into my encrypted files."

"The boy's a hacker?" Tossing the towel aside, Rourke cast a narrow look at the living room doorway.

"Toby is a genius. We don't conduct interviews here. If you can't get our attention, you don't have the brains."

That was clear enough. Disconnecting his phone, Rourke considered his kitchen. A walk on the beach was rapidly becoming more interesting by the second.

The slight grating sound of a computerized printer drifted through the doorway. He really needed a shower but...had that kid said he'd adjusted the satellite dish?

Approaching the doorway felt remarkably like a covert operation. His body tensed just the right amount to heighten his senses. His feet didn't make a sound as he stopped behind the wall before easing his head around for a look.

"Holy Christ!" The living room was Rourke's office. At the moment it had been transformed into some kind of electronic nucleus. Right in the middle of it, Toby sat conducting a symphony of movement. Rourke's own computer had its plastic housing pulled free. There were cables and wires connecting it to the small laptop system that Toby sat punching information into. The printer was still grinding along on some project.

The kid might have been messing with his dish but he also had his own along. Perched atop a bookshelf, a small collapsible dish was aimed out the open window it faced. It was a state of the art piece. Rourke's unit carried a similar one for combat. They weren't even available to the civilian market yet.

"That's for you. Dr. Jasper is sending you a novel on me. He said I could look the Panther over 'cause there's an information lag in the targeting system."

The kid's hands didn't stop while he spoke. Instead they continued punching in numbers and letters alike into the keyboard. He'd switch off to the mouse but return rapidly to the keyboard. It was a frantic pace that made your eyes ache if you watched it too long. But the kid appeared completely in control.

An open box of cereal was shoved off to the corner of his makeshift desk while the trash can was piled high with empty soda cans and crumpled up printouts. The kid's shoes were kicked off in the corner and his backpack was lying open on the floor.

"Have you been up all night?"

"Yeah." The punching and printing continued.

"Geniuses don't sleep?"

That got his attention. He turned a huge grin toward Rourke before he sent his chair across the space between their joined computers. The wheels on the bottom of the chair skidded as Toby ripped the completed pages from the printer's output tray. Another shove and the chair sprang back to his original spot. Toby bounded from it before it came to a full stop.

"Here. Now I'm gonna go tap into the onboard computer system."

Toby shoved the stack of papers at Rourke and lunched himself past him at near light speed. Dropping the mess, Rourke made a grab for the kid but his hand fell short.

"Toby."

"Tobias Kenneth Loren! Halt!" The kid froze in his tracks. Loren stood in the opposite doorway leading to the kitchen with her hands propped on her hips. Rourke's mouth dropped open. She'd obviously jumped right out of her bed. She was wearing nothing more than a tank top and underwear. Little blue lace panties, bikini cut.

"I told you not to get shot while I'm off duty, young man."

"Jasper said I could, Mom!"

"Fine, but you might want to wait 'til Major Campbell tells the armed guard out there that you're clear with him. I'm talking about the guy holding the rifle."

"Ah, sure." The kid swung his eyes back to him making Rourke jerk his own away from Loren's tempting flat stomach. Getting caught looking his mother over made a thin tide of red creep up his neck.

"Why don't you give me a moment to go over this?"

"Okay." Toby reversed course and dove back into the office. The chair sent out a small squeal as the sound of the kid's punching began again.

"Is that normal?"

"For Toby? Yes." Loren had learned to sleep light the day her son learned to roll over. He was a bundle of nonstop action. From toddlerhood to teenager. A second of inattention was an invitation for disaster. Raising her hand up, she rubbed her eyes and forced the last bits of sleep away. Coffee. It was coffee time!

Loren rubbed her burning eyes as she took a deep breath to clear the cobwebs from her sleepy brain. She lifted her eyelids to see Rourke staring at the bare skin her lifted arm gave him a glimpse of across her belly. Male satisfaction was written across his eyes as he caught her watching him and grinned at her temper.

"Pig." The bark of laughter her comment gained almost moved Loren to violence. Glaring at Rourke Campbell and his obvious superior physical size, she flipped around and settled for slamming the door of her bedroom in his face.

Arrogant, lust-driven, crimsoned…pig!

Which could conveniently be rolled up into a single word—man. Maybe male. At the moment, pig just sounded just about perfect.

Loren was going to have bacon with that coffee.

* * * * *

"Mom, is that guy my dad?"

Loren felt her blood freeze in her veins. She'd always known her son would ask about his father some day. In fact, she was amazed Toby had waited this long to ask for some information on his absent father.

"Yes." Turning her face toward her son, Loren picked out the details of Chris that were in Toby's face. It just wasn't fair that biology was dictating that her son look like the man who had abandoned him before he was even born. Chris hadn't wanted his child so it just wasn't fair that Toby was becoming the image of his father.

"Okay." Toby stuck his hands into his pockets and turned back toward the living room. Loren watched him go and felt her mouth drop open. It wasn't supposed to be that simple. She'd expected demands for details and maybe accusations. Instead her ears picked up the sounds of her son resuming his programming frenzy.

"I should break your neck for stealing my son." Chris came around the corner and planted his body in front of her. It was strange the way her eyes moved over him with such calm. The last time she'd seen her husband he'd been in a rage and it had reduced her into a cringing animal that was controlled by fear.

Loren looked at the black spot marking his jaw and felt her confidence grow. She would never give her husband the power of fear over her again. Sticking her chin out she let her eyes dismiss him. Chris' face flushed in anger and he shifted his weight from side to side as he struggled with his temper.

But it was clear that her husband wasn't about to cross his commanding officer by getting into another fight with her. At least not a physical fight.

"I'll get you, Loren, the second you think you're safe." His boots shuffled and he turned away but stopped and sent her a sickening grin. "Then I'm going to watch you bleed."

Loren wasn't afraid of her husband. Not even as he threatened her. But she was afraid of herself. Inside her there was the growing need to avenge herself. She was sort of hoping Chris would make good on his threats, just so she'd have the chance to vent out all of her inner rage.

That was a rather stupid idea. Maybe she had gotten the jump on him last night but Chris was an Army Ranger, for Christ's sake. The fact was, he knew how to kill in more ways than Loren could imagine. Add to that, the fact that the man had a grudge to settle, and Loren really should adjust her thinking.

Dropping her body into a nearby chair, Loren pulled a deep breath into her lungs. Chris should never have discovered Toby. Oh, she knew he'd wanted a son. There had been times she'd stared at her telephone and pictured herself dialing the number that would bring her husband back into her life. It hadn't been easy to be a seventeen-year-old single parent.

But she'd survived. And now Chris knew that the daughter he'd thrown out was in fact the son he'd longed for. Oh yeah, Chris would enjoy watching her bleed. That was for sure.

"What did your husband say to you?"

The fear Loren couldn't find for her husband suddenly twisted her stomach, as his commanding officer demanded his question. Rourke Campbell's green eyes weren't moving over her in desire tonight. Instead, they cut across her face like emeralds. There was absolute purpose carved into the solid stone of his face as he stood over her.

"Answer the question, Loren." She pushed out of his porch chair and moved away from him. Rourke watched her retreat and slowly followed her.

"Nothing important." Loren didn't exactly lie. Chris wasn't important, neither was anything he said.

"Fine, then it won't matter if you repeat it."

"It was personal, Major." The edge of the porch bought Loren to a stop. There was a waist-high railing that she tried to slip past but Rourke was too close for her to do it. He stepped closer and aimed his eyes straight into hers. There was the intense feeling of scrutiny that came with his stare. In fact, it was more like a probe, the way his eyes cut into her face. He reached for the railing and curled his fists around it, forming a cage with his body.

"Tell me what your husband said to you, now."

His words were whisper soft and her skin rose into goose bumps in response. There was such an intense level of awareness that her body had for him. Loren tried to suppress it. Chris had taught her just how dangerous getting close to a man could become. The major here was an animal higher up on the food chain than her husband.

"It's none of your concern."

Rourke kept a careful hold on his temper. At the moment, he was torn between beating the truth out of his man and shaking it loose from Loren. There was something going on between the pair and he wanted to dig it out of her.

It was more than simple attraction now. This close he could smell her sweet flesh. Her chest rose and fell with a rapid rate that lifted the corners of his mouth into a grin. The level of arousal they brought out in each other was just as strong as the night they'd met. It was an intoxicating piece of information.

But nothing would be happening 'til her husband was out of the picture. Rourke focused his attention on the barrier her married state presented. She'd been abandoned at the least. What he wanted to know now was if she'd run away from something.

"Most women don't step out on their husbands when they're pregnant. Why did you?"

"It's none of your business."

"Why did you kick your husband last night?"

"He swung at me first!" Loren spat her response out before she thought better. Horror flooded her as the grin sitting on the major's face widened to show her an even row of white teeth. She'd just given him exactly what he wanted. Rourke Campbell had not witnessed the attack himself and she'd just bet that not a single one of Chris' fellow Rangers were willing to tell their commanding officer that one of their own had raised his hand against his wife.

But now, she'd opened her big mouth and the Major had all the information he needed to open an investigation against her husband. That would be a disaster for her. As long as Chris was out being a Ranger he didn't have the time to bother her. If he got discharged for spousal abuse, well, the man would have nothing better to do than come looking for her.

"Divorce him, Loren."

"I can't."

"You mean you won't." Rourke moved his body closer and listened to the sharp breath she drew. There was a current jumping between their bodies that had his hair rising along the back of his neck. She wanted him and he wasn't going to let her hide behind a marriage that was long dead.

"That's right. I made my mistake and I'll live with it, Rourke."

Chapter Four

She'd called him Rourke.

Staring at his reflection in the bathroom mirror the next morning, Rourke was still grinning. All right, he was acting like a teenager but hell, he liked the sound of his name rolling out of her sweet mouth.

Picking up his razor, he applied it to his jaw with steady strokes. His thoughts were completely centered on his houseguest. That didn't bother him in the least. A man was lucky to have such a lovely woman bunking under his roof, even if she wasn't bunking in the right room just yet.

A slight frown settled over his face. He wanted Loren. The sexual attraction was intensely acute for some reason. The problem was he only had six days 'til she'd be free to head back home.

Now that bothered him. Wiping a towel across his face, Rourke turned toward his closet. Pulling a shirt out, Rourke pulled it over his chest and began pushing the buttons through their holes.

Maybe he should just let it drop. He found Loren too intense. The idea of their relationship ending bothered him. And that was the real reason Rourke should let it go now, before it even got started.

For the first time in his life, Rourke found his genealogy bothered him. He'd always been psychic. His mother was psychic, his brothers were and they lived in complete acceptance of that fact. There had never been a time when Rourke had resented his abilities.

He didn't resent it now. But he was finding it popping up in his mind. Loren was a civilian. His psychic abilities were classified. That meant there was a solid wall standing between the two of them.

Rourke considered the desire that was stirring just with the aid of his imagination. It would seem that the hard facts weren't going to intrude on his attraction to the woman.

But he didn't want the attraction to stop. Rourke was enjoying it. It had been a long time since a woman had such pull on him. In fact, he couldn't remember it ever happening. Six days was a nice long time to explore things.

Beyond that, well, Loren couldn't become aware of who he really was. That was for her good as well as his. But Rourke found himself considering the idea all the same.

It was just possible that a woman who could tackle the male-dominated field of firefighting wouldn't run screaming for a priest the second she found out she'd kissed a psychic.

Even if she had run away from the man.

* * * * *

"Fine! Go ahead and send the local sheriff up here to get me! He'll tell you the same thing!" One of the major problems with a cell phone was you couldn't slam it down when the situation called for it. Just jabbing the off button was rather unsatisfying. Loren glared at the little bit of technology and gave a short hiss.

"Just who is trying to light your temper today?"

Loren jumped. Christ! There had to be a law about a man moving so silently! Her coffee mug went rolling across the kitchen counter leaving a trail of steaming liquid behind. Shoving the phone into her pocket, Loren reached for a dishtowel to catch the spill before she had the added bonus of cleaning the floor to add to her morning.

Rourke folded his arms across his chest and waited. Loren was ignoring him. Her lips were pressed into a firm line as she mopped up the remains of her coffee. She rubbed at the counter 'til it would have passed inspection before giving up and turning her eyes up to his.

"Good morning, Loren."

She should have let the coffee spill onto the floor. Cleaning would have been better than facing Rourke Campbell. There was a heat that rose up her spine every time she looked into the man's face. The kind of heat that got a girl into trouble if she wasn't smart enough to hightail it in the opposite direction.

The problem was, Loren was stuck, stuck, stuck in the man's house for the next six days. His lips lifted into a wide smile.

"I do believe you are blushing."

Loren snapped her teeth together before her mouth dropped open. Oh God! She was blushing. She could feel the heat exploding in her face while Rourke's smile widened.

"I'm just mad!"

"So, I heard." But she was still blushing. "As much as I'd enjoy a visit from my father, maybe I should call and warn him before that call hits his office."

"Your father's the local sheriff?"

"Sheriff Brice Campbell of Benton County. I call him Dad."

"Oh." Loren felt the heat in her face slip away. They could talk about work. It was a nice, safe, sterile subject. "I've got a subpoena for court today and the witness center isn't taking the quarantine any too serious. They think I should show up despite any fatal diseases I might be contaminated with."

"Well, my dad will be happy to set them straight. This area is sealed."

"I imagine that's normal, not just in response to the current problem." That might not have been the wisest thing she could have said. Loren watched the man in front of her as his face went as blank as a granite boulder. Not even the hint of an emotion remained. Loren felt her own lips twitch up into a grin.

"You want to know something, Rourke Campbell? My father was never an officer but he can do that face better than you." Rourke's black eyebrows rose up but Loren decided to finish her thought. "What do you think I am? Stupid? Blind? Or am I just expected to believe most people travel around in high-tech helicopters?"

Loren snagged her coffee cup from the counter and headed for the coffeepot. If Rourke Campbell thought she'd play dumb for him then he was sadly mistaken. Wherever they were, it was classified.

"You can relax, Major. I'm not going to run my jaw, just don't expect me to play the idiot who can't see what's in front of her face."

Rourke didn't just want the woman, now he was getting to like her. He didn't have a single use for a game-playing female. The frank honesty Loren was slapping across his face suited him exactly right. "Deal."

Rourke pushed his frame away from the kitchen counter and poured his own coffee. He sent her a wink before striding out of the kitchen on confident feet.

Loren let her breath out in a slow movement. She pulled another deep breath in and held it.

That had been brazen. Tossing out a challenge like that to a man like Rourke Campbell could have landed her right in a pot of boiling water. Instead the man had taken her at her word. That was nothing to sneeze at. The idea that Rourke Campbell considered her word trustworthy, hit her as a compliment.

He wasn't a man who placed his faith in the undeserving. The same nagging idea to trust the man came floating across her brain. Loren snorted with distaste. That was something that she could never allow to happen.

Wandering out the front door, she took in the morning. Rourke Campbell sure did live in paradise. The huge A-frame house was as sturdy as it was practical. They were surrounded on all sides by forest. The trees stretched up the mountains that were in view. It looked like there wasn't another living soul anywhere to be found.

The cool mountain air was a little chilly as it hit her thin Californian skin. Hugging her arms close, Loren took another sip of her coffee. A duffel bag had appeared with her clothing in it, but her wardrobe wasn't up to the mountaintop location.

Loren shrugged. She'd just have to wear layers. The laundry room might become her best friend, but this was only a limited stay. For now, she intended to enjoy it. Moving away from the house, she wandered toward the three helicopters that sat rather silently in the clearing in front of the house.

Now what kind of a man had combat helicopters sitting in his front yard? It was extremely strange the way the black machines were just there. Well, it was all probably just a precaution against an outbreak of Ebola Tai Forest.

She should have thought of that sooner. No one just took their helicopters home with them. Not even officers.

Well, there was a bright side to the machines being there. Her son was in heaven. Toby was currently sitting in the front of one of the machines with a laptop computer balanced on his knees and wires running down his legs.

Chris' face appeared in the open doorway of the aircraft. The mug slipped from her grip and smashed on the rocky forest floor. Loren didn't care. Chris muttered something and Toby lifted his head to stare at the man. Her son quickly returned to his computer and Chris lifted his face to catch her watching them. His mouth twisted into a sneer before he resumed talking to Toby.

Her hand was frozen over her throat as Loren fought the urge to throw herself between them. She couldn't, mustn't do that. It was Toby's choice. It had to be Toby's choice because it was her fault Chris was his father.

It was horribly amazing the way her adolescent mistakes were affecting someone else's life. Marrying Chris had been immature at the best. Too young to know better, she'd followed her heart right into his arms. But her son was a shiny blessing that Loren would never regret.

Another shiver crossed her chest and Loren abruptly turned around and headed back to the house. No moping allowed! That was one of her absolute rules. No self-pity. No limits. And no MEN!

All she needed was some good exercise. Toby was a great kid and far smarter than she was. He'd make a good choice. Loren raised her face to the morning sun and silently prayed.

Please God, let him be smarter than me.

* * * * *

"Oh, yeah. Now that's a sweet bitch if ever I saw one."

"Grade A ass."

That sort of talk from his men wasn't really something Rourke took extra notice of. Men, his men were rough or they got transferred out of his unit. There wasn't any room for a man that might be too soft. It was just a side effect of their training that none of them knew a thing about manners.

There wasn't any need for social niceties out here anyway. There were never women allowed on the compound. Except today there was one.

Snapping his head around, Rourke fixed his attention on his men. Both Rangers had their field glasses out and aimed at the slope of the mountain in front of them.

"I tell you, Chris is a dumbass. I'd do her a few more times before getting rid of her."

Rourke snapped his head around and caught Loren making her way down the slope. She cut through the forest with steady speed. Her top was marked with sweat from her collar to her waist. She broke through the trees and continued running 'til she hit the house.

Loren didn't let her body quit 'til she heard the screen door hit the doorjamb behind her. Then she bent over and braced her hands onto her knees and tried to breathe. Oh yeah. There was nothing like running to get your mind off of anything and everything.

It was an exercise of will to keep herself from collapsing. There wasn't any room let in her head for emotion turmoil.

A solid grip caught her forearm and spun Loren around like a top. She stumbled before catching her balance. Rourke Campbell's face was etched with anger as he waited for her to steady herself.

"For someone who claimed not to be stupid, you're sure acting like it."

"What exactly is your problem, Campbell?" Jerking her arm out of his hold, Loren propped it onto her hip.

He didn't like her calling him by his surname, but there was a bigger problem to handle first. "Parading around in that excuse for clothing just might get you raped. Those men out there aren't gentle in the least! You're lucky one of the perimeter guards didn't think you were a gift from the tooth fairy."

"If your men are really that barbaric, you have my sympathy. But it's your problem, Major." Loren used her fingers to comb her hair back out of her face. Rourke's emerald eyes were sharp as they sliced at her but she wasn't going to swallow it. "What's the big deal, anyway? Are trying to tell me you guys don't run? I sure thought I saw you in a pair of jogging shorts this morning."

"That's very different, Loren." Rourke let his words out very carefully. He was mad. There was a surge of emotion traveling through his body that threatened to overpower every last ounce of control he processed. One of his men could have dragged her to the forest floor and he never would have known. He wouldn't let her expose herself to that kind of danger again.

"Because I'm a woman?" His head gave a sharp nod and Loren felt her own temper heat up, but this was a battle she was rather used to fighting. Women weren't exactly welcome in the fire academy either.

"Look Campbell, my excuse for clothing just happens to be the fire department approved workout suit. The guys wear it and so do us girls. If jogging is good for you, then it's good for me. I'm not letting my endurance drop during this little vacation." Raising her hand up, Loren stopped Rourke from interrupting her. "And if there's any part of this mountain that you'd rather I stay away from, then you'd better get around to explaining the rules to me."

"This isn't a democracy, Loren, I'm in command here."

"What you are is a chauvinist! You can wear shorts but I can't?" Loren shook her head in denial. "Sorry pal, but I'm fresh out of potato sacks!"

"Fine! You can wear the shorts." She was right. Her dark blue shorts were similar, if not the same as his own green ones. Rourke pulled a solid breath into his lungs and searched for control. She didn't understand the sharp edge his men were balanced on. Nor did she understand the harsh reality of his life.

That nagging thought that had hit him this morning was certainly gaining strength. His life wasn't one a man could share. The plain fact was Loren didn't belong here. All the sexual attraction in the world couldn't change that fact.

For now, he'd better get his ideas out of her pants because it was his fault she was on the compound. That made her safety his sole responsibility.

"You jog with me. Sunup. Don't be late."

Rourke dismissed her. Loren watched the way he turned his body with razor-sharp precision and then he left. His withdrawal was more than physical—it hit her emotionally as well. She'd always been so very aware of him, that right then his dismissal felt very much like rejection.

Pressing her lips firmly together, Loren stared at his bedroom door. She should be happy, at least relieved. The man was finally off her tail and by the feel of things he meant to keep it that way.

Fine... Good... That's way it had to be.

So why wasn't she feeling relieved?

Chapter Five

Loren reached for her toes and ground her teeth together as her muscles ached. Oh…Rourke Campbell was sure a sore loser! Stretching forward she couldn't help but laugh. To be completely correct, she was the one who was sore but Rourke Campbell's pride was so large she couldn't understand how the man walked without his ego tipping him over.

Running with the man had been a pure battle of wills. Loren wasn't sure if she'd won, but she was still standing.

Shaking out her legs, she took a slow turn around the house. Running so hard this morning had turned her legs into Jell-O. She had escaped the muscle fatigue by diving into her computer reports and emails but after sitting at a computer most of the day, the abused muscles of her legs had contracted and turned stiff.

Well, a little walking would solve that dilemma. The sun was sinking below the forest now. All the trees were bathed crimson-gold. Loren pulled the fresh air into her lungs and savored it. The smog in the Los Angeles basin must have made her extra-sensitive to the crisp smell of the mountain air.

Because it even tasted good.

"Your conditioning is good."

Loren managed to keep her smirk inside her mouth as she jumped around to confront her company. The people around here didn't seem to make contact with the forest floor when they walked. That or she needed her hearing tested.

"But then, any female who can become a firefighter would have to know something about endurance."

A pair of emerald green eyes proceeded to run down her body. Loren took in the man they belonged to. He was in prime condition just like Rourke. As he raised his face she noticed the same cut to his jaw that Rourke had. But the way his green stare inspected her lacked the spark of electricity that her body felt every time Rourke looked her over.

It was really annoying to discover that she had Rourke's stare committed to her memory.

"You wear your emotions on your face."

"Most people do." But that was a very strange comment. In fact, If Loren was any judge, she'd say the man was critiquing her. There was a nagging little need crossing her brain to straighten her back in response.

"I'm Loren, and you are?" Loren extended her hand with her greeting but her company simply stared at her hand. He kept his own hands hooked into his belt. His eyes dropped to her hand before returning to her face as he waited to see what she would do.

"His name is Jared."

The pulse of electricity came with just his voice. Loren folded her arms over her chest and tried to force her body into calmness. Her nerves refused to listen. She couldn't hear Rourke coming up behind her, but she could feel him. His face came into view but he was looking at her companion instead of her.

"He's my brother."

"No kidding." Two pairs of green eyes shot straight to her face but Loren simply smiled. "I think I'll just get myself moving before the testosterone levels get to me."

Jared considered Loren as she moved back toward the house and Rourke narrowed his eyes. His brother finished looking Loren over and raised an amused looked at his sibling.

"Careful, Rourke, I'd say you're jealous."

"We're under quarantine, Jared."

Jared grinned and slid another look at the house. "So, don't kiss me."

Rourke raised a fist and sent it toward his brother.

"Hey, if you two are gonna fight, can I watch?" Toby leaned over the porch railing and smiled.

Rourke yanked his arm back and turned toward his young houseguest. Guilt sprang up in response to letting the young teen witness his rather questionable behavior. Jared tipped his head back and laughed. Rourke curled his fingers back into a fist.

"You guys are cool." Toby came down the stairs and grinned at them. Loren did an immediate about-face as her son walked toward Jared. Toby stopped in front of them and studied them with his blue eyes. It was an intense scrutiny that drove home the kid's intelligence level even if it was encased in the lanky body of a teenager. "You know, because there are four of you with green eyes in your family, it throws the average of psychics with green eyes off. Makes the scale look like green eyes are a factor in the level of psychic effectiveness, but you have to discard that kind of data when more than one subject comes from the same gene pool."

"Toby…" Rourke couldn't quite finish his question. The possibility that the kid had crossed into his personal information was too much of a personal disaster for him to absorb.

"You know, I could really show the Army some things on keeping their files encrypted. If you don't keep tabs on the really hot hackers, you're sitting ducks in cyberspace."

Jared shot his hand out and hooked it into the kid's shirtfront. Rourke grabbed his brother's wrist to keep his brother from connecting with Toby's mind.

"Let go of my son!" Loren didn't wait to see if Rourke's brother would obey her. The air was heavy with a hidden threat and she reacted to it on an instinctive level. She wasn't sure just what she was trying to protect her child from, but she launched herself at Jared Campbell before he finished whatever he was doing to Toby.

The man fell back as her body hit him. They went down onto the forest floor and her body snapped as the full current of electricity surged through her. Her vision went black and Loren sucked in a great gasp of air as she fought off unconsciousness. She struggled against the blackness as she forced her lungs to keep working. Her eyelids felt as heavy as bricks as she tried to lift them.

"Aw, Mom. I wanted to feel it." Whatever "it" was, Loren couldn't get her body to stop quivering. It was a good thing she'd pushed both Jared and herself onto the ground because her legs simply wouldn't have supported her. The muscles were twitching and pulsing in an uncontrolled frenzy of movement.

"What is it?" Loren used her temper to control her body. She shoved her legs beneath her and stood up. The world swam before her eyes but she forced herself to stand. Pointing her eyes at her son, she raised a single finger at him.

"What exactly are you trying to discover now?"

"But, Mom… I might never get another chance to meet one of the psychic units. They're way exclusive and totally classified. Besides, it wasn't really hacking. Dr. Jasper said I could look at classified stuff now 'cause I work for him." Toby shuffled his feet and shrugged his shoulders in response to his mother's narrow look. Loren knew that look all too well. There was a definite knack to raising a child with Toby's intelligence level. While a normal kid would experiment with simple rule testing, Toby had to challenge the very boundaries of his nation.

"Tobias, I swear, I'm going to send you to an Amish family for a year! There won't be so much as a single volt of electricity for you to get your paws on, much less a computer!" Loren watched as a kaleidoscope of color began swirling around her head. The more she looked at the colors the less her body hurt.

"But, Mom, these guys are really cool. You should see the file on their mother. Her psychic rating is off the scale."

"Put a cork in it, kid." Jared snarled his order and beat at the dirt that decorated his pants from their fall. Loren held her hand up toward the man. This was a parent's job and she'd do it.

"Toby, there's this idea known as privacy. Digging around in peoples' personal information makes them cranky. When it's classified information, it makes them mad."

"I'm not mad. But I'm going to rip your memory apart."

Loren turned on her heel and faced Rourke's brother. "My son has clearance for classified information but that doesn't mean he has a bit of sense. Judgment is something that only maturity can develop. You must not be a parent or you'd understand how kids can be sometimes."

"I have a son."

Jared Campbell issued that with pure pride. Loren watched him before looking at her son. "Maybe you should find out how he did it first."

"Meaning what?" Jared Campbell crossed his arms over his chest exactly like Rourke did most of the time.

"Well, if a fourteen year old can find those files, sort of makes sense to find out how he did it. Unless you want to take the chance of someone else doing the same thing."

"Excellent idea."

Relief flooded her because Loren wasn't exactly sure just how she was planning on dealing with the man if he made another try for Toby. Desperation had a way of keeping a person running on adrenaline. Once the threat was gone, so was that amazing little chemical.

Loren just didn't understand it. For some reason she was completely bone-tired. Her eyelids were trying to fall closed and she couldn't let that happen. Toby was all she had and she couldn't let anything happen to him.

Where her mind might have been determined, her body wasn't able to keep up. Loren couldn't stop the shrilling colors of that kaleidoscope as it surrounded her and turned her entire world brilliant shades of color. She forgot about keeping her eyelids open. They slipped closed just as her body collapsed onto the forest floor with a boneless grace that only unconsciousness could produce.

* * * * *

"Toby." Her last thought had been of her son, and it was the first word that sprang out of her mouth when she woke up. Loren flung her body upwards and tried to kick the blankets away from her legs. But they were tucked into the mattress of the bed and held against her struggles.

That slight delay was plenty of time for her brain to snap to attention. Los Angeles County ran twenty-four hour shifts for its firefighters. Loren had learned to jump out of her bed and leave sleep behind just like every other member of the department.

Besides, the sight that greeted her eyes was definitely worth her full attention. The wall in front of her was a huge window seat. Just now, a brilliant half moon was hung in the right corner of it. The stars were spread out over the rest of the view and it was quite literally stunning. Loren couldn't remember that last time she'd seen the full brilliance of the night sky. There was too much artificial light in the city and the stars lost a great deal of their luster.

As she'd sat up, the thick comforter that was on the bed slid down to her waist. A wave of steady heat bathed her right shoulder and arm. Turning her head, Loren looked at the fireplace beside her. It was ten feet away and took up most of the wall. The fire had died down but the coals were glowing red.

"Toby's fine."

Loren snapped her head around and found Rourke stretched out over a sofa that was centered on the opposite side of the master bedroom. His bedroom. Her eyes widened as she noted the very masculine color of the bedding she was currently sleeping in.

"Do I want to know how I got into your bed?" Loren slid her eyes back to Rourke and watched the way his mouth turned up slightly into a grin. His eyes moved over her in a lazy movement that caused heat to travel up into her face again.

"I tucked you in, nice and tight."

Rourke showed her an even row of teeth as he said that. He raised his arms and tucked them behind his head. The sofa was an oversized one but he dwarfed it with his frame. His feet were crossed and propped up into the far corner. There was a blanket lying over his legs and a pillow with the same sheeting design pushed under his neck.

He was sleeping on the sofa? Loren blinked her eyes in rapid movement before running them over Rourke again. The man was truly sleeping on that sofa while she was in his bed. That made absolutely no sense. None.

"Why am I in your bed?"

Rourke let out a low laugh. He just couldn't help it. She looked so very...nervous sitting there in his bed. Her pale green eyes were centered on him as she waited to hear just why she found herself in the one place he'd bet she'd never thought to be.

"My room's the only one with a fireplace next to the bed and you are suffering from shock." Rourke lowered his feet and moved off the sofa as he took a moment to assess Loren's condition. She was rosy pink now. But there were black circles ringing both her eyes from the shock his brother's probe had left behind.

Shock? Loren understood that well enough but why had she been suffering from it? Her memory recalled the incident with amazing clarity a second later.

"Where's Toby?" This time, the kick she aimed at the bedding was strong enough to rip it free. Rourke sat on the edge of the bed and settled his hands onto her shoulders, firmly pressing her body back down onto his bed.

"He's asleep down the hall."

"Your brother better not have touched him."

Rourke felt the emotion surging through her and pressed her down again. "Jared didn't know Toby had clearance. He won't bother your son now." Loren settled down and stopped struggling to escape his hold. Rourke savored the moment of acceptance. He liked touching her but their current topic of conversation was a shining example of just why he couldn't let his desire get out of hand. His life was just too damn dangerous for her.

Loren really must have been overtired. That had to be the reason she was enjoying Rourke's hands so much. She could actually feel each and every finger that was closed over her bare shoulders. His hands were far larger than her frame and his grip was draped slightly down her arms. It was a solid hold and she liked it.

One hand moved and traveled down the length of her arm. Loren turned her head to watch it smooth over her skin. The difference in their skin tone caught her eyes as Rourke made the return trip back up her arm. Heat spread from that point of contact toward the rest of her body.

He didn't stop at her shoulder. Instead that firm hand moved up her neck and cupped her face bringing her eyes back to his. The emerald intensity fascinated her. Loren stared into his eyes as she recognized how aggressive he smelled. It seemed to be the very definition of the idea of maleness.

The rough tip of his thumb pressed down onto her lips. The sensitive skin of her mouth felt the calloused surface of his hand. The sensation intensified his appeal, because he wasn't soft. Instead his hands reflected his strength. His hand returned to her face as he settled his mouth over hers. His lips were firm as they gently explored.

The heat rose even higher as it sought out the companionship of his body. Lifting her hands, Loren slid them over the hard planes of his chest and sighed. His mouth trailed away from hers as he moved down the column of her neck.

Rourke pressed her body toward his. There were a hundred places he wanted to taste, one at a time. Moving up, he raked his fingers through her hair. The unruly strands were free and tumbled forward. Twisting his fingers into it, Rourke pulled the scent of it into his lungs. It was the strong scent of the woman he wanted to make his own.

"I want to make love to you, Loren."

Oh God. She knew that. Could feel it, even taste it right at that moment. The husky sound of his voice absolutely terrified her. She just couldn't let a man get so close. Memory slashed across her mind and invaded her body's bliss. The same hands that held so much strength could cause so much pain.

Fear quickly evolved into panic and Loren shoved against her companion. She couldn't, wouldn't survive it again. Not ever again.

Their minds had been fused together as firmly as their bodies. Rourke felt her emotions and struggled to understand them. Emotions were tricky things for a psychic. The streams of sensation were rarely easy to understand, but he understood fear when he felt it.

Loren struggled against his hold as Rourke considered her panic. It was more than her conscience. He'd made that mistake back on the beach. Assuming her reluctance to answer their attraction was due to her morals. Catching the back of her head, he held it steady while he searched her eyes for the answer.

"Easy, Loren, relax."

His voice had lost its husky edge and Loren pushed against his chest to further the distance. Rourke's arms relaxed their hold but kept her firmly within their circle. Loren pressed her palms against his chest as she tried to break that embrace. She could still feel the heat radiating from his chest and she had to move away from it and away from her own female weakness.

"Let me go."

Her words were cut with fear. Rourke felt his face set into a frown as he considered that. Sexual attraction was basic and part of every human on the planet. Puberty unleashed the hormones that made the genders seek out each other. It was society that taught women to associate shame with their sex drive.

Rourke watched the way Loren strained against his hold. Her body twisted just like an animal that was snared in a trap. This was definitely more than Loren's conscience. She was afraid of him. Women didn't fear men unless they learned to the hard way.

"You kissed me, Loren."

Her eyes flew to his face in horror. Loren covered her mouth with her hand and felt her body shudder. She *had* kissed him. The idea rolled over her fear and caused her to simply stare at Rourke in utter confusion. She didn't understand.

"I'm sorry." And she was. Loren stared at the man in front of her and felt herself crumble. Not wanting a man in her life was one thing. Proving that she could make it on her own was important, but had Chris really made it so she couldn't have a man if she decided she wanted one?

She was so tired. Every last ounce of energy she had flowed away from her body, leaving her flesh frail. She relaxed into Rourke's hold because she couldn't hold her body away from his any longer. Her eyes watched his cut into her face before she gave up and let them slip closed.

Everything melted away and Loren went willingly enough into the oblivion of sleep. She didn't have to think anymore. For now, that was enough.

Rourke didn't release her body. Instead he enjoyed the weight of her in his arms. He could still smell her. He let the sensation cross his senses. Desire cooled as his mind searched for the reason behind her emotions. Loren could suppress her natural sense of fear enough to graduate from a fire academy but the idea of having sex threw her into a panic.

That didn't happen without a reason.

Settling her body back into the bed, Rourke yanked the comforter back into place before he returned to the sofa. Propping his arms behind his neck he shifted his mind into sharp focus.

Being psychic was an interesting thing. One major difference was Rourke had explored the human emotion range in more detail than any one person could understand. Emotions themselves fascinated him. The non-logical thoughts could drive men to unbelievable acts of bravery. Emotion could also result in the most brutal of horrors.

The scars that emotional tides left behind, changed people and made them who they were. Loren muttered in her sleep and kicked at the bedding again. Anger crept up his spine as Rourke considered her. Loren wasn't a woman who let fear paralyze her. No, she dealt with her demons and moved on.

Except for one thing. She'd never moved on from her marriage. Instead, she dug a hole and buried it. Suspicion burned through his brain as Rourke considered just why she would have remained married to a man who had left her. Maybe it had been her mother's instinct. If her husband had known about Toby he would have shown up to see the kid.

That made sense. Rourke couldn't help but grin a little. Chris might be his man but that didn't change the fact that he'd deserted his pregnant wife. As far as Rourke was concerned, he'd gotten exactly what was coming to him. No woman should have to put up with an immature husband. They'd been married and Chris should have been a father to his child, whatever the sex.

Ahh, damn it.

Rourke tore his eyes off Loren and stared at his ceiling. She was married! He had to get that through his thick skull. Maybe she wasn't so much afraid of him as she was afraid of breaking one of the Ten Commandments. Adultery was a harsh word even today.

Psychic or no psychic, the brass would skin him alive if they caught him in a relationship with one of his men's wives. So Chris was an ass and had deserted her. That didn't make any relationship between them right.

Even if he convinced Loren to get a divorce that really wasn't an answer. Then what was he going to do? Rourke felt his stomach twist as he considered the fact that he'd have to walk out on her as well. Maybe not right away, but there wasn't any room in his life for a relationship.

Life was handing out harsh lessons tonight. His body was still throbbing with desire as Rourke forced himself to swallow the fact that he wouldn't be touching Loren again. She was a civilian and he had to ship her back to her world before she found out anything else about his.

* * * * *

Waking up had never been so hard before. Loren ran her hand through her hair and pulled on the strands to try and wake her brain up. All she did was make her eyes tear from the pain.

Kicking at the coverlet she wiggled toward the edge of the bed. The thing must have been huge because she was sweating by the time she made it. Her feet smarted as she stood up on them. A hundred needle pricks race along her soles as she forced her body to stand up on feet that had been parallel for too long.

"You just wait 'til I get my hands on you, Jared Campbell." Loren's voice was muffled through her clenched lips as her legs began cramping. She reached into the shower and turned the faucet on before trying to yank her clothing off. Her entire body was stiff and aching from too much sleep. The midafternoon sun was streaming through the bathroom window making Loren issue a low growl at the complete loss of an entire day.

She couldn't remember the last day she'd just slept away. It was an appalling waste of time! "You just wait."

Yanking a sock off her foot, Loren stumbled, off balance, before catching her body.

She glared at her reflection. The mirror showed her a pathetic-looking person. The dark circles sitting under her eyes made her start muttering under her breath again.

At least the water chased the cobwebs from her brain. Loren indulged her aching body in the hot water. She felt the stiffness melt away as she turned so the shower's spray could hit her shoulders.

Stepping out of the shower, she felt infinitely better. Loren grabbed a towel and pulled it across her face. There! Now she was human again!

The refection from the mirror captured her attention again. Her memory was crystal clear now. Loren stared at her eyes and searched her face. There wasn't a single bruise left from her husband's hands. The marks had faded away with fourteen years of separation.

For the very first time, Loren looked at the mental scar she'd carried all those years. Was she really afraid of sex? Maybe it was an absurd question, but she'd panicked in Rourke's arms. While her logical mind told her kissing the man was trouble, that didn't mean that panicking was the answer. Far from it. Loren needed her wits completely in order to deal with Rourke. The man had an amazing ability to reduce her to a pile of emotions.

It was stupid. She wasn't afraid of sex. How could she be? She had a son and the stork hadn't delivered Toby to her. The sexual part of her relationship with Chris had never been the problem. In fact, their hormones were one of the main reasons they'd gotten married when she'd been so young.

Chris had been fresh out of basic training and bigger than life. He'd sparked the very first passion in her young body. But only wives moved onto the base, so they'd gotten married.

It really hadn't been all that original. Half the guys in Chris' training class got married within two months of getting their first orders.

Their domestic problems hadn't been unique either.

Letting a sigh escape, Loren turned toward her clothing. There was no point in riding down memory lane. What was—was. Chris had been a spoiled brat and Loren had long since forced herself to grow up.

She had a lousy husband. Fine. Her fault and she'd moved on. Rourke Campbell made her sweat in places she'd forgotten she had. Fine. That was her problem. Trying to blame it on Chris would be, well, immature.

She needed to funnel her energies into what would do her and Toby the most good. That was the foundation of her life. Focus on the present not the past. Pick yourself up and move forward because no one's life was perfect.

Besides, a good cup of coffee could do wonders for her outlook on life. A sneaky little smile turned up the corners of her mouth as Loren wandered toward the kitchen. Her ears picked up two male voices inside the house. Maybe she'd get the chance to take out her frustrations on Jared Campbell after all.

Loren felt a wide smile replace her grin, as she got close enough to see Rourke and his brother both sharing coffee. In southern California, coffee time was morning. But the brisk mountain weather made it appropriate for the afternoon as well.

Steam was rising from both men's mugs as they continued their conversation. Men had a unique way of socializing. Loren recognized the body language instantly. There might not have been a whole lot of conversation but they were definitely communicating.

Someone laid a fist on the front door with the force of thunder. Both men snapped into deadly form. Loren watched from the hallway as they turned toward the door without spilling a single drop of their coffee. It was amazing to witness the tight control they held over their bodies. It was almost like she understood the difference between civilian and Special Forces at that moment. They men didn't just move, they executed their motions with complete control and precision. There was no doubt in her mind that they could and would use deadly force in the blink of an eye. The fact that they went from the relaxed stance of drinking coffee together to their current positions made it so much more amazing to her.

That same fist pounded on the door again as Rourke caught her with his eyes. His head made a sharp jerk in her direction as he pointed her back the way she'd come. The order was silent but Loren felt her ears ring with it. The absolute authority the man projected had her body responding even before she recognized what she was doing.

Rourke sent her another sharp nod of approval before he took two long-legged strides and jerked his front door open. Not the way she would have done it. Rourke didn't stand in front of the open doorway. Instead he sent the door swinging inward while his body was against the wall.

"I want to see my wife!"

Even knowing Chris for the spoilt brat that he was, Loren was still surprised to hear exactly how belligerent he'd decided to be with his commanding officer. She stepped toward the door and caught the harsh look Rourke leveled at his man.

"You seem to have forgotten how the Army works, soldier."

Chris raised his chin and tried to out-bluster his superior. Rourke didn't suffer the insubordination for long. He grabbed the center of Chris' shirt and flung him back out the front door. Loren ran into the kitchen but came up short as Jared stepped into her path. The man literally used his body as a solid barricade to keep her from following the two men out onto the porch. Loren bounced back and immediately tried to go around the man. But she didn't have to. A split second later and Rourke had pushed Chris down the steps and into the clearing in front of the house. Jared moved with his brother in almost perfect synchronization, following Rourke as he kept her behind his body.

Loren followed and found Rourke's brother purposely blocking her path again. The man stepped in front of her as she tried to move around him. The look he cast over his shoulder was just as full of authority as his brother's had been. Loren felt her pride bristle but clamped her jaw shut. Rourke had enough trouble to deal with at the moment.

"She's my wife. Sir!" Chris spat the expected title of *sir* and stumbled back from Rourke's frame as he tried to shove his commanding officer but found Rourke immovable.

Loren had decided back on that beach that Rourke looked untamed. Right now she was certain the man was completely uncivilized. His body stood with tightly controlled aggression. The type you saw in a wild predator. Chris' eyes went large but he refused to back down.

"There's no married housing here." Rourke used a tightly controlled voice with his man. He could smell the liquor on the man. But that didn't make Rourke angry. Far from it. Chris was digging his own grave with his insubordination and Rourke would be happy to watch him do it. There was no place for Chris in his unit. This little alcohol-sponsored incident would just save Rourke the trouble of kicking the man out.

"Even a Goddamn officer can't just screw around with my wife! I want a divorce." Chris sneered in contempt before he raised an arm and pointed at Loren. "And I want my kid too! You're an adulteress and I'm going to get custody of my son."

"I won't live with you." Every head turned as Toby popped up from inside one of the helicopters. The three black Panthers were sitting at rest in the center of the driveway and Rourke had driven Chris toward the aircraft.

Toby jumped down from one Panther and stood facing his father.

"You're a minor and my son. That bitch poisoned you against me. You'll see, just as soon as we hang out together. You'll see."

Toby regarded his father in silence before he raised his blue eyes toward Loren. Her son sent her a wink as he stuffed his hands into his pockets and turned back toward his work. Toby jumped back into the helicopter and picked up his laptop computer again.

"Toby, you're my son and you'll do what I say!"

Chris didn't know he was fighting a lost battle. When Toby decided something wasn't worth his time, her son was oblivious. Toby promptly began punching lines of code into his keyboard.

"No court will give you custody of me. You tried to kill me before I was born." Toby raised his face and glared at his father. "My mom almost died trying to keep me alive. That's all I need to know."

"That's bullshit! She's a liar."

Toby pegged his father with a clear face. "The interesting thing is that Mom never said a word to me about you. So, I decided to look around and find out. The sheriff's department has a big file on you. I saw what you did to her with your fists."

Loren felt the blood drain from her face. Every pair of eyes turned toward her but she didn't care. Her son looked at her and simply grinned. Her hand rose to cover her mouth as the simple truth hit her.

Toby had hacked into the Pentagon, hacked into NASA and he'd hacked into the sheriff's department files too. When she'd refused to have an abortion, Chris had resorted to drinking first and then he'd tried to beat her badly enough that she'd miscarry his unwanted daughter.

Chapter Six

"Why didn't you tell me?"

Loren felt her muscles tense. Rourke was using the same low tone he'd used with Chris. Moving her eyes around, she studied Rourke's face.

But he couldn't hide the anger in his eyes. Loren rolled her shoulders and tried to relax. Her lips felt parched and she ran her tongue over them. Rourke's eyes immediately focused on the telltale sign of her nerves.

"There was no reason."

"Wrong." Rourke crossed the kitchen and pulled Loren out of her chair. He handled her with extreme care but firmly pulled her body toward his. He had a deep need to touch her right then. Feel her skin and assure himself that she was well. Pulling a deep breath into his lungs, he enjoyed her scent and the pulse it triggered in his body.

Loren just couldn't deal with that attraction right now. Her mind was full of too many memories. She needed space and Rourke was just going to have to give it to her.

"Let me go, Rourke." Loren placed a single hand onto his chest with her words. She didn't like the fact that she wasn't in control of the outcome of her request. If Rourke decided he wasn't releasing her, she wouldn't be able to free herself.

He gave her exactly two feet. But he propped himself at an angle against the kitchen counter that blocked her solidly against the wall.

"Did he try to kill you?"

That was a question Loren had rolled around inside her head for years. Sure, it sounded simple enough but it certainly wasn't. Admitting Chris had tried to kill her was also admitting that she'd made a horribly wrong choice in just who she took into her heart.

That was a mistake that could haunt a woman's soul forever. If you were so very wrong in choosing one man, how could you ever make the decision to take another man into your bed?

Loren fixed her eyes on Rourke. If she admitted to being so wrong in her judgment on Chris, then her current attraction to Rourke would have to be questioned too, maybe even rejected.

She cringed as she considered that idea. There was something about Rourke that just felt so secure. Every time she looked at the man she felt more of that pull. Weakness and desire was eating away her self-discipline.

But there was definitely one thing she would not do, even for Rourke Campbell.

"Forget it."

Loren was too quick. Rourke felt his anger tense because she'd homed in on the true reason for his question. He just needed to hear the accusation from her mouth. If Loren would point the finger, he could do something. Until she did that, Chris was an innocent man because she had not named her attacker. The detective who had written the report had suspected it was her husband but there was no evidence without Loren's statement.

"All right." Rourke crossed his arms over his chest and considered her. He wanted Chris and he was going to get him. If Loren wanted to play hardball, that would have to be the game. But there wasn't going to be any getaway for her bastard husband.

"Since you don't seem willing to let Chris have what's coming to him, maybe we should let him have it his way."

A tingle crept up her spine as Loren's eyes flew to Rourke's. The expression aimed at her made her feet itch to move back even though she had no room for retreat.

Rourke unfolded his arms and felt his emotions surge. Letting go of his discipline was intensely enjoyable. "Chris wants to divorce you for adultery. But you're not guilty of that. Yet."

Composure went flying right out the window. Loren felt every nerve ending snap a second before she tried to dive around Rourke. She didn't make it even half a foot. The man was truly the predator she'd sensed. He pulled her out of her steps and wrapped her into a solid steel embrace against a chest that was completely unyielding.

But she wasn't scared and that was the worst part. Loren felt a moan rise out of her mouth as her body begged her to surrender.

It would all be so much simpler. Chris would be gone and she wouldn't have to worry about fear keeping her from moving on to another man. She wanted Rourke in a painful manner, nothing mattered but the desire burning her alive. Her body was straining toward him because they weren't close enough. There were too many barriers between them. His shirt hid the warm male skin she craved to touch. She wanted to rip his shirt away until her hands could touch and feel the hard strength of him.

Whatever her reasons, Rourke didn't care. He could feel her surrender. Her breasts pressed against his chest as the nipples stabbed into him. Her hips tipped forward in blatant invitation and he just didn't give a damn anymore!

He carried her toward his room and kicked the door shut with his foot. Her eyes were glassy as she stared at him. Rourke took a long look in their simmering pools before he lowered his mouth to hers. Passion didn't disappoint either of them—it was searing hot in its intensity. He laid her in the center of his bed. He stood for a moment as her eyes traveled over his body. Need was written across her face as he reached for the buttons on his shirt. Rourke pulled his shirt off and tossed it across the room.

His hands were impossibly hot on her skin. Her top didn't last more then a few seconds as he striped the garment from her. Loren watched the way he smoothed his hands over her breasts. His fingers gently rolled her nipples and sensation centered on the single point of touch. Rourke moved his hands to cup each breast entirely before moving back toward her nipples once again. The bed moved as he climbed onto it and knelt over her. His knees spread right in front of her, teasing her with the thick bulge of his pants.

There was such heat in the touch, but there was infinitely more. Rourke wanted to love her. It went so much beyond sex. This wasn't some groping frenzy that would crescendo in a frantic pounding of genitals.

It could be so deeply right. But it wasn't. Not this way.

While he cradled her breasts, Loren cupped the sides of his face and raised it to hers. His eyes burned with passion but that didn't hide the sheer enjoyment he was experiencing. The man wanted to touch her. It burned out of his eyes as she held his face. It lacked the stark selfishness of lust. Instead the need blossomed up in full three-dimensional colors.

Rourke absorbed the last few seconds of sensation before he pulled his hands away from temptation. He wanted her intensely, but she was right. Sitting back onto his knees he considered her as she lay in his bed. The globes of her breasts gleamed against the navy blue of his sheets. Her nipples were beaded into hard little nubs that his mouth was watering to taste.

And he was going to get that taste. "One way or another, Loren. Right here in this bed, I will have you. Soon."

* * * * *

"No self-pity" was definitely one of her rules, but Loren didn't think it applied to contemplating her temptations. Twenty-four hours later she was still thinking about it. Well, him. Them. Loren just didn't know anymore.

It was just possible she was one of the stupidest humans on the planet. Rather ironic when you coupled that with Toby's intelligence level.

At thirty years of age, you'd think she'd have managed to gain some level of comfort with her own sexuality. All Loren felt was the awkwardness of inexperience. Her breasts were still sensitive. Of course that might just be due to the fact that all she'd done all night long was dream about Rourke and the way he'd run his hands over her.

Her head was killing her and there was only so much help that a girl could expect from coffee. Loren rubbed her forehead but headed back to the kitchen for another cup of coffee anyway.

Her cell phone rang, piercing the silence. Loren reached for it happily. Maybe her real problem was boredom. Four days on this mountain was getting old. There was a limit to the amount of e-mail she received. Even the spam ads were looking interesting this morning.

Nothing but static came through the phone. Loren jabbed the off button and went toward the kitchen. Most of her calls came through as static. The military element surrounding her seemed to cut the satellite signal on her civilian cell phone. She was even in the mood to listen to her mother tell her how wrong she was.

Pouring the steaming coffee into her mug, Loren smiled as she caught the rich aroma. Rourke Campbell sure did know the value of good coffee. His kitchen didn't stock the bargain stuff, no sir. It was pure Columbian roast. There were about fifty firefighters in Los Angeles who thought lousy coffee was a test of manhood.

Stepping onto the porch, Loren considered her son. Toby was still infatuated with the Panthers. That wasn't something to worry about just yet. In fact, Loren found herself rather grateful for the aircraft. When Toby got bored, it was best to run for cover.

All manner of interesting things tended to happen when her son was searching for something interesting. Things like, the FBI showing up on your doorstep. Toby had hacked into too many top-secret files to count, and he was rarely caught. It had been a relief when Dr. Jasper caught her son. The NASA scientist had a lot in common with her son. The man had given Toby direction.

Movement caught her eye and Loren turned toward two of the Rangers who were standing guard. A third was slowly moving toward her. He walked with the heavy steps of a dying man. Loren knew the walk instantly. It was a shuffle and pull, like the person was trying to wrench his body away from the ground.

His face was chalk-white. He had every piece of gear strapped onto his back and his eyes stared forward. He shuffled again as his fellow Rangers noticed him but they didn't break through the man's shock.

"Don't touch him." Loren issued her command as she stepped out of the man's path. Bright red blood ran down his checks just like tears. His teeth were stained red. He stumbled forward again and stopped directly in front of the house. His arm moved up and cut a perfect salute toward the front door before he dropped to the ground in a boneless pile.

The Rangers moved forward and Loren launched herself at them. Surprise gave her the ability to shove both men off their feet. But that same fall took her down with them. One solid fist hit her jaw and her head snapped back with the blow.

"He's infected." Both men looked at their comrade before they began cussing. They gained their feet in a split second before moving away from the fallen man. Loren was yanked off the ground by her forearms and sent after the retreating Rangers. She didn't have to turn around to know just who was tossing her around.

Rourke stood looking at his fallen man. His stance was stiff as his face fell into the granite mask military men adopted to deal with death. Loren moved back, because there was a certain level of common respect you gave to a commander when they were losing one of their own men.

Cal Worth was dead. The horrible reality of the disease hit Loren as she looked at the body. It was eighty percent fatal. The worst part was how little was really known about Ebola Tai Forest. The best doctors on the globe thought it had to be spread by fluid contact with an infected person. But that was based on limited data.

Loren wasn't interested in becoming some of that needed data. Her eyes looked down at the bunkhouse the men used. It sat three hundred feet from the main house. The front door was open and Loren could see the blood smeared on it from Cal's hands. No one had been watching the ranger and he'd gone back into the familiar building in the last hours of his life despite the fact that he'd been sleeping in a smaller bunkhouse on the north side of the compound. With no solid evidence of infection, everyone had fallen into a false sense of ease over the past couple of days.

Her eyes flew toward the ground and searched for any drop of that same blood. The forest floor didn't display any but the man had been bleeding out and his contaminated blood could be anywhere.

"Burn it." Her words were ignored by the Rangers. Loren looked at Rourke and caught the harsh glitter of his emerald stare. "Burn everything. Anything he touched." That was the only way the Africans said the disease could be stopped. Entire villages were torched to control Ebola Tai Forest. Rourke considered her before nodding his head with agreement.

"Pendergast, which bird was Worth in?" Authority radiated from Rourke as he took charge. His men fell into absolute obedience.

"Sandy." The female name didn't surprise Loren. Pilots had an unspoken need to name their aircrafts after women.

"Strip the live ammo and get the other two off the ground. Toby, close up and get out of that helo."

"Yes, sir."

Loren was surprised to hear her son snap to attention but his timing was impeccable. This was a race for their survival. Either everyone on the mountain worked together or they might very well all die together. Toby's youth wouldn't protect him.

"Loren, go up to the house." Protest sprang up instantly. Rourke's eyes caught it and issued a clear warning. "You're bleeding."

Her hand flew to her face and caught the wet slide of blood. The Ranger who had hit her began cussing again. He was inspecting his hand with intense scrutiny. Loren pulled her hand away and let the blood flow. If there were any germs on her face the last thing she wanted to do was press them into the torn tissue that was bleeding.

"Put a cork in it, Wenton. The lady saved your hide by knocking you over." Ranger Wenton snapped his mouth shut and took a long look at Loren. His eyes lost their cutting edge before he dropped his hand and gave his complete attention to his commanding officer.

Loren turned toward the house. There had to be obedience now. If not, suspicion could have everyone at each other's throats long before the disease could kill any of them. The very fact that this was a unit of Army

Rangers made that threat all too real. Every man here had more than just one gun. The horrible possibilities that panic could produce turned her blood cold.

Her cell phone buzzed again and Loren reached for it out of habit.

"Loren?" Her feet stopped in their tracks because she was afraid of losing the satellite signal. Her father's voice was just barely making it through the static.

"Dad? I'm here." And she desperately wanted to hear her father's voice. There was a harsh reality that it might be the last time they spoke.

"Is there any proof of the disease?" Loren felt a hollow laugh rise out of her chest. Her dad could gather more information than anyone she knew. It was amazing how he knew stuff the second it happened. Her silence was all the confirmation he needed. She heard the curse he didn't try to muffle.

"Hang tight." The line went dead and Loren turned the phone off with a frown. That was her dad for you. It was all business, all the time. She marched into the house and toward the bathroom.

The mirror showed her a split lip. Loren reached for hydrogen peroxide and didn't wince from the sting. Instead she welcomed the sharp pain. The sting gave her some small assurance that germs were being killed.

Smoke drifted in from the open door but that didn't give her the same confidence. Instead the harsh smell only deepened her concern. They could burn the disease out of the worldly belongings but they couldn't stop any infection that was already moving through any of their bodies.

Cal Worth was now the main source of concern. Any man who had been in the same helicopter with him could be infected. Any one of them could have infected any of the others.

And if Chris had become infected, her husband could have infected Toby.

Loren stepped toward the open door and watched Rourke command his men. Her stomach twisted as she watched him walk over ground that could be laced with infected blood. He didn't flinch. Instead he stepped forward and loaded another pair of fuel cans into the one Panther that was still sitting in the front driveway.

He looked over the interior of the aircraft before he turned away. He stopped thirty feet away and pulled his gun out of its holster. He leveled the black pistol at the fuel cans.

"Fire in the hole." The sharp pop of the gun hit her ears a second before the fuel cans exploded. Orange flames shot out and ripped the helicopter apart.

Watching the million-dollar machine burn should have made her mourn for the tax dollars that went up with it. Instead Loren was worried that they'd waited too long to sterilize any potential threat it might have posed.

Chapter Seven

The house was silent again. Loren wandered toward the front windows and looked out at the scorched earth. The metal hull of the Panther was still sitting where it had burned. Beyond that the blackened skeleton of a bunkhouse marked its final moment.

Every inch of ground had been burned. It was shocking how complete the Army personnel had been. The house was spared only because it was Rourke's personal residence and the soldiers were never allowed inside.

But it was clear that the house would be torched the second there was any hint of further infection. The harsh sound of a flamethrower hit her ears. They were still burning the earth down the hill.

Twenty-four hours of nonstop burning. She should have been more used to it. Brushfire season in southern California meant weeks of fires, but the constant smell of burning leaves and fuel still turned her stomach.

Loren watched the teams stop their work. It was easy to see them. The hazardous material team had helicoptered in within an hour of Cal's death. They wore complete environmental suits with their own, clean air contained inside a tank on their backs. It drove home the frightening reality of their contamination.

A helicopter came over the house and the windows shook. The remaining team members made their way toward it. They were slow and clumsy in their inflated and insulated yellow suits. The last man climbed aboard and the aircraft lifted away.

So now they were left to wait it out.

Time could move at a snail's pace when the mind was so full. Loren tossed her head and used her fingers to comb her hair back. The sound of Toby punching at his keyboard touched her ears and she smiled slightly.

Her son had promptly gone into the den and calculated their odds of possible infection. He'd presented his numeric possibilities to her with an adolescent grin.

Ah, to be a teenager and invincible!

Loren turned and dropped her cup. She jumped back out of sheer shock and Rourke reached for her forearms to keep her from hitting the wall.

"Could you breathe heavy if you're not going make any other sound when you move..." Loren snapped her mouth shut. The man in front of her was exhausted. Heavy fatigue was carved into his face. It was clear he hadn't slept.

"Dad will appreciate the compliment. He taught me to be light-footed." Rourke let his words come out slowly. He wanted to just look at her and burn her face into his mind. Loren was so alive. Her light green eyes glistened and shouted her energy at him. Reaching forward he gently smoothed his hand over her check. Her skin was silky and warm.

"I'm sorry, Loren."

He left on silent feet a second later. Loren felt her composure desert her because she just felt him like he was a part of her. There was an urge shouting at her to follow the man and lift some of his guilt away.

She stood in place instead. Truth had a way of hitting you right between the eyes when you finally got around to facing it. The truth was she wanted to be with that man. To yank his clothes off and let him do everything his male instincts told him to do with her.

Facing her own mortality must have emphasized just how precious time really was. She'd been tossing away opportunities. Right now, Loren was looking at a clock that just might be winding down for her.

But it wasn't her own death that was really bothering her. It was the idea of Rourke's death. He had always been so strong. He still was. Even with fatigue trying to drag him down, the man was still completely virile.

As silent as the house was, Loren found herself paying attention to her steps as she followed Rourke. Every tiny sound she made seemed as loud as thunder. She wasn't sure why she was following him, but it just felt right.

She came to a sudden halt in the hallway. Rourke had left his door open. The master bedroom door had never once been left open. Today it was. Stepping forward she caught the sight of Rourke lying on his bed. The thing had been huge when she'd been laying in it. But it was the right size for its owner.

Rourke had laid down, boots and all. His feet were crossed at the ankles and his arms were over his chest. Loren let her eyes slip over him as she looked at the body that he had such complete control over.

She couldn't remember the last time she'd just looked at a man for the sake of seeing him. Heat rose in her cheeks and she enjoyed it. Loren felt other signs of arousal invade her body as she looked at his firm lips. It was very freeing to have the opportunity to just let her curiosity run free without the worry that his emerald eyes would catch her.

There was just something about his direct stare that made things permanent. She could let the small signs of passion move over her skin right now because Rourke wouldn't see them. If he caught her eyes right now, there wouldn't be any denying her rather basic yearnings. Rourke would peg her dead straight and her body wouldn't help her conceal the truth.

Loren leaned against the doorjamb and let her eyes slide all the way down his chest to his abdomen. His legs were powerful, just like his arms. Her lips went dry and Loren let her tongue run over their surface before she pushed away from the doorway and walked toward her own room.

Her body protested the entire way but she went. Loren ran her hand through her hair and sighed.

Rourke heard the feminine sound and curled his fingers into fists. He wanted her. Even now, as the hard truth was hitting him, he just didn't care. He could smell her delicate scent coming from the guestroom and all he wanted was to pull her clothing away 'til he found the source of the scent.

It was basic and primal and all-consuming. Rourke let his eyes close again. It was a damn good thing he was so tired or Loren wouldn't be sleeping down the hall any longer.

* * * * *

Her nap wasn't restful. Instead Loren tossed around and woke up tired. Her head ached but she got out of bed. The sun was setting as she made her way down the hall.

Right about now she was remembering why men were such trouble. Passion made the body unpredictable and Loren liked her neat, organized life. Keeping tabs on her son was all the excitement she needed.

She stopped and stared at the closed master bedroom door. Loren had to really think about the afternoon's events. Had she just dreamed it or had that door really been open? Her headache doubled and she shook off her ideas.

"You are truly an addict, Loren."

Another mug went toward the kitchen floor. This time it was full to the brim with steaming coffee. Loren yelped as it splashed onto her bare feet. She was plucked off them a second later and deposited on the kitchen counter.

Rourke muffled a comment before he flipped the faucet on and eased her skin under the cold water. Her feet were covered with pink splotches. He looked at the marks and muttered again.

Damn it! He was just trouble for her.

"So, where's the bubble bath, Campbell?" Loren waited for Rourke to look at her before she burst out laughing. In his haste to attend to her burns, he'd managed to soak her to the waist. Water was dripping down the cabinets and pooling on the counters because he kept turning her body about to ensure that he didn't miss a single tiny bit of the burn.

Rourke aimed his emerald eyes at her before he looked over the mess he'd made in those thirty seconds. Loren continued to laugh as his face took on a devilish look. One hand held her in the sink as Rourke lifted a coffee mug from the counter and filled it with cold water.

Loren's amusement died immediately. Rourke aimed the cup toward her head and she thrust her hand out for protection. The water splashed up and out of the cup and onto them both.

"It's cold, Campbell!"

His own laughter joined hers as Rourke tried to keep her squirming body on the counter while he also tried to refill the cup. "I noticed. But you needed a good cold bath a couple of hours ago, lady."

Loren went deathly still. Rourke returned her stare and waited. She was just so shocked to discover her own longings. That reaction was a mystery to him. They were both healthy adults, more than past the age of consent. Yet Loren faced her desire like a virgin on prom night. So surprised to discover it inside her own body.

"You knew I was there." Loren shook her head. "Of course you knew I was there." Loren had just forgotten to consider what her son had told her.

Psychic.

Now that was a huge idea. In a really weird way, maybe it made things make more sense. Rourke had always been dead-on with understanding exactly how she was feeling. The question was, was it pure male instinct or something altogether different.

"Only because I heard you moving down the hallway."

Loren watched his eyes as he said that. The man was waiting for something. She wasn't sure just what. She didn't doubt his words. Rourke just was more in tune with his sense than any man she'd ever known. Besides, dishonesty was a notion she couldn't apply to him.

It just felt wrong.

"Okay." Loren made a grab for the cup and snagged it away from Rourke's distracted hold. She tossed the whole load at his face and laughed as the cold water ran down his chest.

He pressed his lips together as his eyes glowed with the promise of payback.

"Hey, Mom, the R.O. girls are, like, going nuts trying to find you."

"I'll be right there!" Loren shouted her reply and prayed her son wouldn't come looking for her.

"R.O. girls? What's that? A club?"

"Yes." Loren tried to escape his embrace but he held her in place with a single raised eyebrow.

"What does it stand for, Loren?"

"You're nosy, did you know that?"

"I pay attention to details." He held her in place as his eyes dropped to her lips. Loren felt heat snake through her body as his head began to lower.

"It stands for restraining order."

Rourke's face reflected his surprise and his grasp eased as he tried to decide if she was joking or not. Loren wiggled off the counter and flipped Rourke a smirk.

"What in the hell kind of club is that?"

Loren shrugged before edging toward the kitchen door. "Sounded better than 'men are pigs'." He growled at her and she hightailed it into the office and her son's presence before Rourke got the chance to cross-examine her.

Rourke watched her go and let a frown slip over his face. The impulse to just lay it all on the line was strong.

He wanted to know just what she'd do when faced with the reality of his psychic abilities.

Rourke turned around and began cleaning up their mess. Exactly what was he thinking of doing anyway? Tell Loren he was both psychic and permanently in the Army?

There was one great idea. Toby had already told her that fact but announcing it to her would force her to either accept or shun him.

The little matter of quarantine would make that rather hard to live with. He'd find himself bunking out on the forest floor with his men, because he sure as hell wouldn't let Loren toss a sleeping bag down next to a single one of his Rangers. If she was determined to separate herself from him, he wouldn't put it past her to camp out in the Washington mountains.

But the second possibility was what bothered him the most. It was just possible that Loren would take it in stride.

If that happened, temptation would have him in its claws. Loren would be in his bed so fast she wouldn't have time to protest.

Letting her go after that was going to be the worst ordeal he'd ever endured. Rourke was certain of it.

So, why in the devil did he keep thinking about it?

* * * * *

Her cell phone was missing the next morning. Loren stared at the empty bedside table and felt her temper rise.

That man moved too silently, too quietly or she was getting old and feeble. Raising Toby had taught her to sleep light. One single sound from her son normally brought Loren to full attention.

Oh Lord.

Loren dropped her head back onto her pillow. This was rapidly getting beyond any sort of control. She could try and reason it out but there was a plain truth that was getting too large to ignore.

Trust. Even faith. Rourke Campbell made her feel secure.

That scared the absolute hell out of her. How could something like that happen? It was continuing to grow with every little look or word that the man gave her. Sure, he was still in the mood to pursue her but even his method made her more at ease with his approach.

Loren felt him herding her into place and there wasn't a single thing she seemed to be able to do about it. His net was far too effective. But it was more than that. Having the man close to her was pleasant. It was even becoming comfortable.

Which was why he could walk right up to her bedside without her moving a muscle. Pushing her body up from the bed, Loren headed for the shower. Turning the puzzle around in her head was going to give her a migraine.

She was attracted to the man and her common sense was useless.

Her shower took less than four minutes. Tension was running her in circles today. Loren looked out the window before walking toward the kitchen. It was too quiet this morning.

There wasn't even the scent of coffee in the air. Loren stopped and considered the kitchen counter. The coffee was sitting there and the pot was next to it. Both had been abandoned.

Her neck knotted into cords because Rourke was a detailed man. He'd been called away and the reason might very well be a case of further infection. Loren turned on her heel and left the house.

She wasn't going to wait. Something was happening, she could actually feel it floating on the morning air.

"Go to hell, you pup. If I was going to kill you, you'd be dead." Loren recognized the voice instantly. Her eyes flew to her father's face as he argued with two of Rourke's Rangers. Loren blinked her eyes rapidly and tried to make the sight of her father standing in the front yard dissipate. Not here. Not right now. Her dad just couldn't be here.

But he was. Rourke had taken up his normal stance with arms crossed over his chest as he considered the intruder. Two of the Rangers held her father under guard and true to his nature, he was amused.

The Rangers held their automatic rifles in her father's face but he was ignoring them. Instead he was standing in a rather arrogant stance as he faced off with Rourke.

The horrible reality of her father's presence impacted her a second later.

"Dad, you've got terrible timing."

"Lavender, that's no way to talk to your father." Loren bristled and her dad grinned. He hated her name more than she did. He turned that grin toward Rourke and eyed the younger man thoughtfully.

"Well, now. I don't care just who your mama is, young man. It doesn't give you the right to take off with my family." Her father considered Rourke and pointed a firm finger at him. "Looks like we got us a real problem here."

"The problem is yours, old man." One of the Rangers spat that out as he angled his weapon into her father's face. Loren held her ground because she knew her dad just a little too well. That Ranger was about to catch hell.

The younger man never saw it coming. Her father gave a half-turn away from the man before his boot was thrust into the Ranger's midsection. He went flying as her father plucked the weapon from the man's grasp. He tossed the rifle at Rourke before turning toward his victim.

"I had my tabs before you stopped thinking your mama's tits looked good. Your perimeter sucks and maybe you better stop calling me an old man because I walked right through your unit."

And that was her dad. Loren felt the slight laugh escape her mouth because she just couldn't help it. First, Sean Loren would have to be dead before he ever forgot to tell another Ranger that he had his tabs. The Ranger patch known as tabs could only be earned by completing an intensive extra training program. It was an elite group and her father was one of them.

Rourke turned and caught her amusement. His face was stone-hard but his eyes were sparkling. There was an admiration sitting there for the older man's skill that all the rules in the Army couldn't dismiss.

"You've got tabs?"

"Hell, yes." Her dad smirked at his guard as the second man lowered his rifle. "You think I learned how to break your line anywhere else?" The older man gave the two Rangers back their pride with that statement. Being bested by another Ranger was acceptable.

"Get over here and give your daddy a hug."

Loren propped her hands onto her hips instead. She was going to choke on the testosterone fumes for sure. "Dad, we are under quarantine. The last thing I need is for you to be infected."

"Life's a real bummer sometimes, my girl."

Rourke just couldn't help laughing. Loren was so damn cute when she was frustrated. She raked a hand through her hair in agitation and pressed her lips together. A solid whack landed on his shoulders and sent him forward a half step.

"Oh, pardon me, sir. I'm getting clumsy in my old age. That's my little girl standing right down there."

Rourke glared at the man as he lifted one gray eyebrow and smirked at him. The heavy hand of parental authority was sitting on the man's face. It was aimed right at Rourke. Loren was right—this guy had to go immediately. Getting around Loren's barriers was plenty of trouble. Rourke didn't need her father here critiquing his performance as well.

His border patrol came up the drive and they stepped aside to let the two Hummers by. Loren's father took the moment to grab his daughter in a bear hug. She wiggled away and glared at him, but her light green eyes were sparkling.

Loren finally gave up and smiled. Her dad was…well, her daddy. He gave her a wide smile in return. "Now, that's my girl. Where's my grandson hiding?"

"Holy shit!"

Loren went flying back as her father shoved her away. Chris had jumped down from the Hummer and never got another word out of his mouth. Chris hadn't taken the time to see just who was hugging her, but Sean recognized his son-in-law instantly.

Her father attacked the man with pure deadly intent. He tossed Chris right over the hood of the Hummer and dove after the man. Loren was powerless to stop her own stumbling fall right into Rourke. He lifted her off her feet and set her aside before he launched himself into the fight.

It took Rourke and three of his Rangers to drag her father off Chris. Her husband was flat on his back in the dirt and gasping for breath as Rourke dragged his opponent away.

"I've waited fourteen years to choke the life out of you." Her father's face was glowing with primal rage. Chris struggled to his feet and stepped away from the man.

Loren just couldn't take it anymore. It was her life! She stepped in front of her father and stuck her finger into his face. "Take a number and get in line! If anyone gets to kill my husband, I do. So just back off, Dad."

Her father went deathly still in response. Loren tossed her head before she turned around to look at her husband. Maybe being stuck on this mountain was a good thing after all. It was time to deal with her past mistakes.

"You want a divorce, Chris? Fine. But you'd better be real careful how you word it."

Chris sneered at her as he tried to recover his pride. "Just what the hell are you going to do about it?"

"Touch my son and I'll kill you myself."

Chapter Eight

The words were final. Loren couldn't take them back and the absolute truth was, she didn't want to. She turned her back on Chris and never looked back.

It was long overdue. Finally letting her marriage go was the last piece of emotional baggage she'd been lugging around. The weight on her shoulders felt incredibly lighter. So, she wouldn't know where Chris was anymore. That was a flimsy reason anyway. If the man truly wanted to come looking for her, he would find a way.

The truth was, there had still been some small part of her that actually clung to the idea that Chris thought about her at all. The harsh truth was, the man didn't care about her and hadn't spared her a single thought since he'd walked out on her.

Well, now she was letting it go completely.

Or was she? Loren stopped in her room and walked into the bathroom to look at herself. Was it really all behind her? The image of Rourke holding her breasts sprang up with crystal clearness and she felt the same panic come with it.

Pulling her shirt over her head, Loren unhooked her bra and dropped it onto the counter. The air hit her bare flesh and brought a heightened sensitivity with it. She watched her nipples lift and bead. The really strange thing was Loren couldn't remember really looking at her body in the last fourteen years. In fact, she always had her clothes laid out before she ever got into a shower.

She'd been hiding from her own insecurities. Rejection left its scar on every abandoned wife and she wasn't any different. She'd just never faced it.

Suddenly, Loren was impatient with herself. She didn't like being afraid. One thing being on her own taught her was to look every last bit of trouble straight in the face, because then it could be overcome.

Unzipping her pants, she tossed them aside and pulled her panties off as well. Considering her reflection, Loren let her eyes wander over every inch of herself.

She was pretty. Every man might have a slightly different view of just what "beautiful" might be, but she wasn't unattractive.

"You're stunning, Loren."

Of course Rourke had followed her. Maybe she'd been expecting him. Loren didn't care. She watched him through the mirror. Confidence surged through her because there was more than common lust written on his face. Loren turned to face him because she wanted to see his eyes.

Watching passion flash from his emerald eyes, things were completely clear. This man was going to be her lover. Her flesh was demanding it and Loren accepted the fact that her common sense would have to yield. Rourke was simply watching her as she finally understood.

He didn't want to just take her. This man wouldn't accept anything except complete compliance. Every little touch had been a clever move of seduction. Compliance of the flesh was one thing, seducing the woman took true strategy.

"Come here, Loren."

"Not yet." His jaw clenched in response and Loren felt his anger zip across toward her. She lifted her chin with firm resolve.

Rourke wasn't accepting that. His hands closed over her wrist with a grasp of solid steel and yanked her into his embrace. Her bare skin registered the hard reality of his male body as he very deliberately wrapped his arms around her to trap her against him. Loren settled against him without complaint. She watched his eyes flash in triumph before he lowered his head to kiss her.

He took his time, sliding the tip of his tongue over the smooth surface of her lips. Loren gasped as sensation curled inside her belly. He caught the sounds as his mouth took possession of hers, tasting the depths of her willingness. Her hips thrust forward with need and found satisfaction in the hard presence of his sex.

"Wait."

"Why?" His voice was rough and low. His fingers moved over the side of her face as Rourke waited for her reason. The man was a hairsbreadth from losing his control. There wouldn't be any waiting if he did that. It was amazing to think that they had been throwing water at each other just a few hours ago. Rourke had a playful side that only emerged when he felt at ease. It was a compliment that he'd shared that playtime with her. Loren raised her own hand and laid her fingers onto his firm lips. They were still moist from her kiss and she shuddered as she forced her passion aside.

"You would never have an unfaithful woman. I don't want to cheat in your bed."

"Chris might be your husband on paper but he sure as hell isn't your man, honey. He crawled onto top of you like a raw kid, didn't he?"

His arms tightened. Loren shivered as his words reminded her of her rather disappointing wedding night. Between the pain of virginity and Chris' rough handling, there was nothing in the memory that inspired passion. Sex was simply… blunt.

Rourke slid one hand over her bottom to firmly squeeze one of her cheeks. Her belly tightened with acute sensation that settled directly in the center of her sex. It was a surge of pleasure that fed on his touch. Her flesh was pulsing with need.

"We were both kids. There wasn't any shotgun at our wedding. I grew up and left my excuses behind a long time ago."

His head dipped in a solid nod. "You belong to me, Loren, and I won't wait much longer. Divorce him or I just might kill the man myself."

He left her and Loren sank to the floor. She was boneless without him and she curled into a protective ball as her enflamed flesh screamed in protest.

Maybe she was walking down the wrong road again. She dropped her head to her knees and felt the slide of tears. Even if she was making another mistake, Loren didn't think she had the will to stop herself.

And even if she did, Rourke would slice through the barrier in seconds. He'd have her and then he'd leave her.

There was no other possible solution.

* * * * *

He was in a dangerous mood. Rourke knew it. But he let the animal inside himself loose today. It was the only thing keeping him from dragging Loren off to his room. He let that idea bloom in full vivid color inside his mind. Her body bare and writhing against his sheets as he sank into her center. His staff was rigid as he savored the idea of thrusting into her body and watching her face while he did it.

His teeth clenched and Rourke smiled. Raw desire was coursing through his veins. There was something inside him that enjoyed the primitive need pulsing through his body. Seducing a woman certainly held its rewards, but right now he wanted to capture Loren and ride her 'til she sobbed with rapture.

The soft sound of his printer stopped. Rourke eyed the neat pile of crisp sheets in the output tray and curled his lips back. He stood up and grabbed the papers in one fluid motion.

Loren was at her normal spot in his kitchen, right next to the coffeemaker. She was gazing out of the window, her mug of freshly poured coffee forgotten on the counter top. Steam rose from it as she continued to contemplate the view. Rourke dropped the papers in front of her and caught her shoulder as she jumped.

"You'll never hear me coming unless I want you to, honey."

Loren lifted her eyes to stare into the ruthless ones of her host. Rourke Campbell's face was etched with primitive aggression that made her belly curl with excitement. The need to yield to him was becoming painful now. Inside of her was a woman raging against the bounds of a dead marriage that she forced herself to hide behind. His green eyes bored into hers as his hand tightened on her shoulder. He stroked her face with a single finger while he let his eyes settle on her mouth.

"Sign them." His words were whisper soft. He was daring her to refuse his demand. Moving her eyes away from his face she looked at the kitchen counter. The neat stack of papers was already filled out and ready for her signature. Somehow, Loren had never thought that dissolving a marriage could be reduced to a thin pile of computer-generated forms.

She spun away from his hold. She couldn't look at either Rourke or the papers. Both glared at her, highlighting her shortcomings.

"I'm going for a walk."

Loren hated the fact that she waited for Rourke to nod his approval before she turned to leave.

"Loren." His voice was still soft. She barely looked over her shoulder because there was far too much promise in his voice. The need to run was climbing up her spine as she felt the walls of the house contract around her. His green eyes almost glowed as she felt him sink straight into her mind. Loren wavered slightly as she felt his desire collide with her own inside her thoughts 'til they mixed into a potent combination of overwhelming need.

"You have exactly one hour."

She sprinted out of the kitchen door like a rabbit. Rourke frowned as he watched her go. There were parts of him that could scare the strongest man half to death. He prided himself on keeping that side of his personality hidden. Baring it to Loren was a test. He raised his wrist and noted the time.

Now all she had to do was find the courage to come back and face him. The psychic and the man, she'd accept them both if he had to run her to ground.

* * * * *

She wasn't dressed for running. Loren stopped before she'd even crossed the driveway.

Psychic.

The man was really a psychic. She felt the corners of her lips twitch up into a little smile as she considered the idea. It didn't strike her as odd. In fact, she wanted to ask him at least twenty questions about his abilities. Her curiosity was raging as she tried to decide exactly what he'd done to her in the kitchen. She'd felt his mood. It was like they were plugged into the same current of electricity.

Her feet carried her as Loren let her ideas wander. She let a silvery laugh escape her lips. Rourke's audacity really should have rubbed her wrong. Her divorce was her decision but she was still tingling with sensation as she thought about his determination.

Her husband moved with the same quick reflexes that Rourke did. One second she was along with the forest. The next instant Chris was glaring at her as he stood directly in her path. His face was a mask of granite but his eyes were strangely unfocused, like he couldn't quite decide what he was thinking about.

"You should have told me about my son."

"If you'd been in the delivery room with me, you'd have found out at the same time I did." Loren took a long look at Chris before she noticed the lack of manhood in him. He was just as immature as he'd been the night he'd left. "Don't blame me for your lost chances. You walked away from us."

"You never used to be such a bitch."

"Yeah. I was a real pushover. I should thank you for the lesson in life."

Chris' eyes locked with pinpoint sharpness on her face. His mouth twisted into a mask of rage as he lowered his rifle toward her chest. "Think you're smooth, don't ya? But if you're dead, Toby's mine. Don't matter if we were estranged or not."

He wasn't bluffing. Loren knew the look in his eyes just as intimately as she knew her own face. His hand flexed as he settled his finger along the trigger of the weapon. Anger rose up inside her as she recognized just exactly how vulnerable she was. But she wasn't going to stand there and take it!

"Want to shoot me, Chris? Fine. But the only target I'll give you is my back."

Loren spun on her heel to present her back as the only target. "Somehow, I don't think anyone will buy the excuse about self-defense if I'm bleeding out from my back!"

Her body twisted into a tight knot of tension as she waited for Chris to respond. There was no doubt in her mind that he truly wanted to shoot her. But he didn't want to get caught—it was the only defense she had. Seconds crawled by as Loren firmly forced herself to begin walking back toward the house, with her chin steady and her eyes looking straight in front of her.

Two shots pierced the air and Loren felt her body jerk with them. Time froze as she waited for darkness to enfold her. Her ears heard each and every sound of the forest. She could smell the dirt her own footsteps had sent up.

She felt her lungs expand with a breath and time rush forward with the simple motion of life. There was no pain, no blackness. Spinning back around she stared at the crumpled form of her husband. Bright red blood leaked from his head in a slow stream even as his fingers clutched the trigger of his gun.

Death was always silent. Loren blinked her eyes and searched his chest for movement. Rourke exploded inside her mind a second later. She stumbled as the man brutally thrust his presence into her consciousness. She felt his body bearing down on her with an intensity that lodged her breath in her throat.

But her eyes were glued to Chris as the trickle of blood continued to flow down his face. The horrible reality of that scarlet trail twisted her gut. Murder was a terrifying thing to add to the mountain's quarantine. Everyone was locked on the property until the disease was completely stamped out.

"Loren?"

Rourke caught her arm as he broke through the forest. He swooped down on her like a raptor, his eyes just as keen as a hawk's. The emeralds searched her face before rising to look behind her. His face fell into a solid stone mask as his finger bit into her arm. The curse that slipped out of his mouth fit the moment extremely well.

"What happened?" Rourke shook her as he demanded his information. He firmly invaded her mind. It was completely overwhelming. Loren frantically shoved against his body as she felt her senses being ripped into.

"Get out of my head!" He seemed to control every thought and feeling inside her brain. Loren shivered violently as she struggled to maintain her grip on her own control.

"Why?" Suspicion laced his voice but he released her mind back into her own control. Loren gasped for breath as she rubbed at her temples. She struggled to think beyond her own fear.

"What don't you want me to feel, Loren?"

The suspicion coating his voice made her furious. The harsh look on his face made her shove away from him. Curses sailed across the forest as more of Rourke's men responded to the sound of weapon fire. Their ears were tuned to listen for it far more acutely than her civilian ones.

"Loren, what happened?"

"I don't know."

Rourke snorted. He curled his fingers into tight fists that turned white at the knuckles, betraying his urge to grab her again.

"My back was to him."

That made too much sense to Rourke. His body tightened as he considered the angle of his fallen Ranger's rifle. Loren's green eyes were filled with anger that was just too intense to dismiss. His men's curses gained heat as they stood over their comrade.

"Get back to the house."

The urge to proclaim her innocence bubbled up inside her chest. Loren clamped her teeth tightly together. She had nothing to prove. For heaven's sake! She was the only person present who didn't have a gun. She refused to start babbling like an idiot.

Turning her back on Rourke she kept her chin in the air as she left. Tears pricked her eyes as she walked faster and the house came into view. It shouldn't matter what anyone thought about her. Chris' buddies could curse her 'til doomsday. That didn't change the fact that someone else had pulled the trigger.

But Rourke Campbell's suspicion stung. It was cutting into her heart. Silent tears leaked from her eyes as she hurried into the house and down the hall to hide behind her bedroom door. A relationship wasn't worth a wooden nickel without trust.

Rourke couldn't possibly trust her if he could suspect her of murder.

* * * * *

He was already on the edge. Rourke felt the surge of emotion hit him as Loren's scent drifted away on the afternoon breeze. He tightened his grip on his control as he battled against the danger of making snap judgments.

He had a dead man. The gunshot wound made it a direct result of someone on the mountain. Adding murder to the current level of stress promised an explosion if discipline wasn't absolute.

Rourke faced his men with deadly focus. They snapped to attention as he moved to stand over the body. It was a clean shot. It was also a common round of ammunition that had made the wound. Any of his men could have fired the round. Any other person on the mountain could have gained access to their weapon's lockers.

"Burn the body, Sergeant. Immediately."

"Sir?"

"You heard me. That blood could be infected. The quarantine orders stand."

"Yes, sir."

Rourke considered the hard looks of his men as they backed away from their comrade. "Search the area for any weapons. If you find something, don't touch it."

Their replies of "Yes, sir" betrayed their hunger to uncover some incriminating evidence. Rourke didn't wait. There wouldn't be anything to find. The accuracy of the hit betrayed the shooter's skill. He'd cover his tracks, Rourke would bet his oak leaves on it. That left them to suspect each other of the deed.

It left him with exactly one barrier left standing in front of claiming Loren. Rourke cursed under his breath as he considered the obstacle. It would be so damn easy to reach into her mind and make sure. The subconscious only held the truth. When he sank into another person's mind, deception coated his own mind like tar.

Toby stood on the top step of his house with his hands pushed into his pants pockets all the way to his forearms. It was strange to see the youth standing so completely still. His eyes were lifted to the forest where a thin taper of black smoke was just beginning to rise above the treetops.

Rourke cleared his throat as he considered the task of telling the boy that his father was dead.

"Gramps told me. I just wanted to make sure it was true."

Toby's face was twisted with an angry grin that made Rourke stop. The kid wasn't sorry his father was dead. Resentment shone in his eyes as he watched the smoke rise. Guilt crept up his own spine as Rourke considered just how little sympathy he had for man in question. An officer cared about each and every man under his command. But the flat truth was Rourke didn't care this time. Chris had finally pushed someone too far. The harshest part of it was Rourke had been getting dangerously close to the line himself.

Letting his eyes drift over Toby again, Rourke looked at the young man Loren had raised. He was a good kid. Parents passed their weaknesses on to their children. It was a cycle that few people ever rose above. Loren had. The proof stood there in the firm set of her son's shoulders as he refused to hide from life's harsh realities. Toby was too honest to fake grief for a father he'd never known. Even to get attention. Most adults couldn't resist the need to be the center of attention, even if it was for the wrong reason.

Loren's appeal became hypnotic. There was a pull radiating from her that snaked out to clutch his body. Rourke curled his lips back and enjoyed the rush of sensation. It traveled along his skin as the nerve endings pulsed with sharp sensation.

There was nothing in his way.

It was a potent drug. Rourke felt his sex rise into painful stiffness. Morality didn't intrude with another man's name because being a widow meant she was fair game. Instead, Rourke considered the afternoon sun and just exactly how many seconds there were until dark. Duty still clung to his shoulders. Abruptly turning away from his house, Rourke headed toward the weapons bunker. He was in charge until nightfall. The duty rotation applied to every single man on the mountain. Including himself.

The urges inside him collided with civilization's boundaries. He wanted to drag her off to his bed and he didn't much care what the rest of the world thought about that. Rourke shook his shoulders as he felt his erection swelling painfully inside his pants. His skin screamed for freedom. Just as the male inside him demanded satisfaction, the need to mate pulsed through his blood as he considered the approaching night.

* * * * *

"I'm gonna get some sleep, Mom."

Loren swung around in a split second. Her son reserved that phrase for when he was ready to drop from exhaustion. His brain would drive him for days on end. Toby didn't seem to be able to shut it down enough to sleep. He'd work straight through 'til his body dropped from fatigue. Sometimes he simply slumped over his keyboard.

Toby shuffled his large feet as he headed toward the room he was sleeping in. His sneakers squeaked on the hardwood of the hallway because he didn't have the strength to lift his feet into steps any more. Loren followed him and watched his body with a critical eye. She'd caught him more than once as his body simply collapsed before he found a bed.

"Night, Mom. I love you, ya know."

Loren didn't say anything as she stood in the doorway. The bed sent up a groan as Toby fell onto it. He rolled onto his side as his lungs began the deep breathing of sleep.

A silly smile lifted her lips as she closed the door behind her. Neither of them grieved for Chris and he was the one who lost in the equation. Freedom settled onto her shoulders making her feel as light as a ballet dancer on her toes.

Her eyes fell on the closed door of the master bedroom. Temptation was thick and swift as she moved toward that doorway. Loren let her fingers trail over the polished surface of the door while her mind offered up detailed images of the room's master.

She shifted away as heat snaked up her belly. Darkness invaded the house. Loren let her fingers travel down the surface of the hallway wall as her eyes tried to adjust to the absence of light. She searched for the light switch.

Instead of the cool plastic face of the light control, her fingers found the soft fabric of clothing. It was warm from its wearer. Her fingertips registered even the deep rhythm of Rourke's heart.

She knew it was him. He floated around her and across her mind in a blanket of sensation that she was woven into. His fingers stroked her face, making goose bumps race down the side of her neck. The touch was intensely hot as her eyes caught only the barest of shadows to mark his position.

Details didn't matter so much anymore. Rourke wouldn't be near her if he really thought she was a killer. Beyond that, nothing mattered but the needs clawing at her body and the fact that she was free to feed her cravings.

Those fingers brushed along the column of her throat as she raised her head to offer the tender skin to his touch. His hand traveled onto the fabric of her top and she groaned as they were separated by the barrier. Her skin screamed for bare contact but sensation still gathered under his touch as he brushed his fingers across her collarbone and lower to the swell of her breast. The nipple lifted beneath her top, beading into a hard nub that raised the fabric toward his fingers.

A tiny gasp escaped her lips as he caught her nipple between his thumb and finger. Rourke absorbed the sound as he rolled the point. She was frozen in her steps as she considered her options. Curling his hand around the globe of her breast, Rourke gently squeezed it. Her scent drifted up as her body heated. His penis hardened in response to the musky smell of her sex. It escaped through the layers of her clothing making his nostrils flare in primitive reaction.

"Did he make it to the bedroom?"

The concern in his voice made her shift away from his touch. She'd always been alone in the role of parent. The fact that Rourke took notice of Toby made her nervous. There was a depth of intimacy there that she'd never shared before. "Don't." Loren tossed the word out like a barrier.

Rourke drifted across her mind in a steady glow of heat as he surrounded her in the small confines of the hallway. His fingers curled around her chin to raise it up. Her eyes didn't show her anything but blackness, but she could feel him along every inch of her skin. There was the soft sound of his breathing but she felt his eyes touching her face.

"I'm sorry, Loren."

Her chin was suddenly free. Somehow he was able to see in the pitch blackness. Rourke captured her wrist in a solid grip before walking by her. He pulled her behind him as he shouldered the door to his room open and spun her through it with strength that made her tumble forward.

"Sorry about what?" Loren snapped her question. Her heart was lodged in her throat as she eyed the shadowed outline of the master bed. She turned abruptly to face Rourke as he slowly closed the gap between their bodies.

There was a tremor in her voice that made Rourke pause. She shifted her weight from one foot to the other as she eyed him with slightly large eyes. Starlight poured in from the ceiling, bathing her in its silvery light. He pulled a deep breath into his lungs and savored the heavy scent of her.

She was a widow. Toby was sleeping and Rourke flatly didn't care what anyone thought about it. His body pulsed with the need to claim her. The waistband of his jeans was painfully snug across his swollen penis.

"That I'm not giving you any more time."

"You don't look sorry." He looked hungry. Loren felt it in the deepest part of her belly. Her womb twisted into a knot as she felt the slick glide of fluid inside her passage. She gasped with the acute sensation. He hadn't even kissed her. But her body was desperate for his.

His lips curled back to show his teeth. "You're right, honey. I don't give a damn about what anyone thinks. I didn't on that beach and I still don't."

But he did care about her. Loren sensed it as he stood his ground instead of rushing her. Overpowering her body would be simple for a man his size. Instead he seemed to be waiting for her to adjust to his presence. Loren unconsciously rubbed her bare arms. Gooseflesh had risen along them as she watched the flare of heat in his eyes. She felt so cornered but what made her wary was the burning enjoyment that rose up in response to his possessiveness.

"I'm not on any birth control." Loren blurted it out like a shield. The smile disappeared off his face right before Rourke captured her. His arms closed around her, trapping her against his powerful chest. His mouth dropped onto hers with ruthless demand as he thrust his tongue inside to taste her. His hands cupped her bottom, lifting her to fit against the bulge in his pants. Loren whimpered as she fought the urge to wrap her thighs around his lean hips and cradle that hard flesh right in the center of her body.

"Take your clothes off, unless you don't care what I do to them." Rourke whispered his words against her ear. She shivered in response. He nipped the soft skin of her neck before lowering her feet to the floor. Her hands were twisted around his shoulders and trailed over his chest as he let her down.

She didn't want to stop touching him. Loren let her fingers rest on his chest as she tried to remember why she needed to pull her hands away from his body. All she could think about was the way his skin smelled. Just the deep heady scent of him and the way he felt under her hands. She didn't care anymore. She found a button on his shirt and pushed it through its hole. Hair sprung up from his bare chest as she moved to the next button and freed it. Loren smiled with satisfaction as the shirt fell away under her deft fingers. She pulled on the open sides of the garment to free it from his pants. A deep rumble of approval shook his chest as she rose on her toes to push the open shirt down his shoulders.

He smelled so incredibly strong. Loren threaded her fingers through the mat of dark hair exposed to her. It was springy and full. She found his flat nipples and rolled them between her fingers exactly the same way he'd handled her own. Her breasts swelled with the memory as she felt her nipples tighten even further.

She was unbearably hot. Her shirt scratched her skin. Rourke's hands smoothed over her neck making her lift her chin with delight. The contact of bare skin to bare skin was pure pleasure. A tiny purr vibrated up her throat as his large hands stroked down her neck.

Rourke ripped the garment off her. His hands hooked into the neckline and jerked. The buttons gave loud pops as they scattered and fell to the floor. Loren gasped at the abruptness of the motion. Rourke's control over his strength was amazing. He knew exactly how to apply it. She let her arms fall away from his chest as he stripped the shirt down her arms. His hands went after her bra.

"I'll do it." Loren sprang out of his grip as she fumbled with the hooks on the undergarment. It was the only one she had. Parading around the male population of the mountain without one made her protective of the garment.

His eyes watched her. Loren grasped the bra to her breasts as she watched the intensity of his eyes. His fingers flexed as she slowly lowered the bra a millimeter at a time. Feminine power flooded her as she watched his teeth bare in response to her teasing. The fabric caught on her nipples making them tighten with sharp sensation.

"Drop it."

Rourke growled as he watched the scrap of lace flutter away from her body. Desire was raw as it pulsed through his body. Her nipples were swollen tight with invitation. Pulling a deep breath into his lungs, Rourke caught the smell of her sex. The two steps she'd retreated were too far. He reached for her waist and lifted her 'til her breasts swayed in his face. Clamping his lips around one tight bud, Rourke pulled it into his mouth to taste.

His lips were scorching. Loren moaned as the tip of his tongue flicked across her nipple. Pleasure traveled in a direct line to her belly making her passage clench with need. She felt so empty. Her body was incomplete. He held her by her waist as he released her breast and sought out its twin. Tasting and licking, his arms didn't even tremble as he held her up for his pleasure.

Rourke growled deeply as he licked her nipple a final time. Moving forward, he didn't lower her body until his bed was waiting to catch her. Moonlight spilled in through his windows and onto her body. Rourke reached for her waistband and pulled the snap open before he grabbed the bottom of the garment and stripped it off her body. The crotch of her panties was dark with moisture. Rourke stared at the stain as he worked the buttons on his fly open.

Loren felt her eyes grow round. She clamped her teeth together as he dropped his pants to the floor and stood proudly before her. He was magnificently bare and completely sculpted to perfection. His sex stood forward in a swollen rod that looked impossibly large. But the walls of her passage ached with the need to grasp his length.

His fingers twisted in the thin scrape of fabric that shielded her from his eyes. Rourke pulled the panties down her legs as he watched her face struggle with temptation. Need and desire mixed together as she dropped her eyes back to his erection. But she rose up onto her elbows as his body made her wary. It was a reaction he was used to. He'd polished his exterior for years but under the exterior was the hunter he'd been trained to be. When he mated, he captured, and he intended to take Loren.

A tiny curl of fear hit her as Loren watched Rourke's face. Need was pulsing with desperation through her blood, but the raw hunger reflected from his face made her wary. She rolled away from him. The bed bounced as he came down across it. A solid arm clamped her in place as his body pressed along her back. The contact of bare skin was intense. She could smell the heated aggression radiating from him. Firm lips landed on her neck making her whimper as her nerve endings erupted into sensation.

"Shh…"

Enjoying his touch was a bad idea. Loren knew it but she couldn't stop herself from arching her neck. Rourke trailed tiny bites down her neck as she heard her own throat release a moan of approval. His body felt so incredibly solid behind her. Secure and warm in a way she couldn't remember feeling before. His hands turned her 'til she lay flat on the bed again. Lifting her eyelashes, Loren stared into Rourke's face as he propped himself up on an elbow.

She raised her hand to trace the hard angle of his jaw. The skin was tough and slightly rough with a day's growth of beard. Hunger rushed into her as she used her entire hand to smooth over his face again. This was a man. In the deepest part of her she recognized his superiority as a mate. The female inside her craved him with stunning force.

A deep groan rumbled out of his chest as Loren yielded to him. Rourke couldn't think beyond the need anymore. She pressed toward him as her hips lifted with invitation. The scent of arousal flooded his senses as her thighs gently parted. Cradling her head in his hand, he took a deep taste of her mouth. Her tongue thrust hesitantly toward his as she followed his lead.

Later, he'd taste every inch of her. Need pulsed across his brain reducing him to the most basic of levels. He rolled over her as he caught the strands of her hair in his grip.

He still controlled his strength. Loren felt the tremors shaking his limbs as he kept his needs from turning brutal. His hips pushed her open. Spreading her flesh as the tip of his weapon probed for entry. The hard thrust of his body made her cry. Her passage stung as it stretched to admit him.

"You can take me, honey. Relax." Elation swept through Rourke as he listened to her moan. Pulling his hips back he thrust forward into her depths 'til her flesh gripped his entire length. Her passage pulsed around him as she shifted beneath his body. She was as tight as a virgin. It pleased the hell out of him even as he battled against the raging need to pummel her body 'til he erupted inside her.

Reaching between their bodies, Rourke found the soft folds of her sex. He spread them 'til her center was open to his thrusts. She gasped as his movements rubbed the sensitive bundle of nerve endings.

Loren felt the pain vanish with a single thrust from his hips. He pulled back and she shoved her pelvis up to capture his staff. Pleasure spiked through her as he buried his hardness inside her. Everything fell away as she matched his rhythm and clung to his shoulders.

Her body clenched and tightened 'til it exploded. Loren felt the walls of her passage grip his staff as she tried to hold him even closer during her climax. Rourke didn't resist. Instead he plunged his penis deep inside her as he growled against her neck. She felt the deep spurting of his seed as it hit her womb.

His arms clenched as he held her beneath his body. The harsh rasp of his breathing matched her own as their bodies strained toward each other in the final moments of intimacy.

Chapter Nine

She should feel guilty. Loren looked at herself in the bathroom mirror. She felt a lot of things but guilt was not one of them. The room was lit only with moonlight. But the silvery cast was plenty to see with. The master bathroom was large with two sinks and a double mirrored front closet.

Her nipples were still beaded. Loren shifted as her body ached. Her clothes were scattered all around the bed. She watched the deep rise and fall of Rourke's chest before she reached for a towel and wrapped it around her body.

She needed to think. Her body was still radiating with the remains of pleasure from his touch. Her passage ached but was still wet and sensitive. As she walked, the folds of her sex rubbed against her clitoris, reminding her of just how intense her climax had been.

Loren set her feet down silently as she walked back into the room. Nothing stirred as she let her eyes linger over the man sleeping there. His chest and arms were sculpted to perfection. Temptation urged her to drop the towel and rub against that firm muscle. Loren moved toward the door instead. She couldn't listen to her impulses.

The doorknob turned silently. There was a tiny click as it opened and Loren wrapped her fingers tighter around the knob to pull it open. Rourke's hand landed on the door right in front of her eyes and kept it closed. His breath hit her ear as she felt the very distinct touch of his staff against her bottom.

"I'm tired, Rourke, I want to go to sleep."

A sharp tug sent her towel toward the floor. His large hands closed over her hips as he lifted her feet off the floor and turned her to face him. Loren frantically grabbed his shoulders as she was lifted like a child. Rourke moved between her thighs as her back ended up against the door. Her thighs eagerly wrapped around his hips as his hands cupped the cheeks of her bottom.

"You can sleep right here in my bedroom." The hard head of his sex probed her body. Loren gasped as she felt her body open for him. It was pure reaction. Once again her body sent fluid sliding down the inside of her passage to welcome his body. His eyes watched her intently as he very slowly thrust the head of his sex into her. She hung there as her body closed around his. Her breath rose from her chest in tiny pants as she yearned for him to fill her completely. His hands cupped her bottom and held her absolutely still while his eyes continued to watch her.

Her body quivered but Rourke waited. His staff was aching with the need to thrust into her body but he wanted her to demand it. She tried to tilt her hips but he held them firmly in place.

"Say it, Loren, tell me what you want."

His voice was rough with demand. His hands were ruthless as they gripped her and kept her from completing the possession. Loren clenched her teeth together as she refused to surrender her will to him. His jaw tightened before he lifted her off his length. Loren felt the loss keenly as her passage clenched painfully.

"All right, Rourke." The three words sounded like a surrender to her ears.

"All right, what?"

There wasn't any kindness in his voice. Loren shivered as she contemplated just how basic their attraction was. Their bodies clashed against each other with a force that ripped away every hint of civilization. Right here it was male and female drawn together by the need to mate.

Wrapping her legs more firmly around his hips, Loren leaned toward his neck. She nipped the firm skin that covered his body before she licked the spot and moved slightly further up his neck. Her fingers were splayed across his shoulders, absorbing the immense strength of her companion. He issued a low grunt of approval before letting his sex probe hers again.

His thrust was smooth and slow this time. Loren felt his body quiver as he controlled the possession. Her body stretched around him as her hips encouraged deeper probing.

She felt too good, too hot, too tight. But Rourke didn't care. His body demanded more and he thrust into her with a rhythm that made her body submit to his. Her hips tipped forward with surrender. He growled approval as he listened to the tiny sounds of pleasure coming from her throat.

"Look at me, Loren."

It was a final intimacy that she resisted. Loren squeezed her eyes shut as she felt her climax peaking. His body stilled as his demand hung over her head. She needed to move but his hands held her captive.

"Loren, let me see your pleasure. Share it." His voice was a dark whisper that drew her in like an addict. Lifting her eyelids, Loren gasped as he forcefully thrust his body into hers. Sensation broke like a wave as his eyes sank straight into her soul. They became one person in that moment as she felt her body clench around his and the deep jerk of his sex as it pumped his seed into her.

His lips landed on hers in a delicate kiss. His tongue traced her bottom lip before he caught a deeper taste from her mouth. He turned away from the door and walked back toward his bed with her still joined to him. It didn't matter. Her body lingered in the ripples of pleasure that were born deep inside her satisfied body. Feeling him wrap his frame around her felt so complete. His arm bound her across his chest as he arranged her head onto his shoulder. Their legs twisted as Rourke pulled one of the sheets over her body.

Rourke watched her sleep. From somewhere inside him came the need to just watch her. His body was too aroused for slumber, his staff still hard. The sweet smell from her body kept his aroused even after taking her twice. He smoothed a hand over her back as she shifted in her sleep. Her head lifted and he pressed it back to the center of his chest. Loren was exactly where he'd been picturing her since he'd first seen her. She was staying there.

Lifting his eyes, Rourke caught the stars and their position. He knew the night sky intimately. He could find his direction or the time just by looking up. Right then, he noticed just how few hours there were between holding Loren and daybreak.

Sunrise would bring reality crashing down on his shoulders. Taking Loren to bed wasn't going to win him any popularity points with his men. Rourke didn't care. There was always a degree of distance that a commander kept from his men. But that detachment wasn't going to solve their murder.

His mountain was loaded with suspects—including the woman in his arms. Smoothing his hand over her head, Rourke considered her face. It would be very simple to probe her mind, seek out any guilt that might be buried inside her. But the truth was, he didn't want to know.

So at sunrise, Rourke Campbell intended to find his murderer. He was going to spend the rest of the night hoping the trail didn't lead him back to Loren.

* * * * *

There were too many minutes in an hour. Loren rubbed her forehead for the hundredth time and tried to find some diversion from her thoughts. Nothing surfaced in her fatigued mind to rescue her. Tension was knotted around her throat like a noose.

She gave a dry laugh at that idea. There was more than one person who would love to see a noose around her neck today. The cutting looks coming her way from Chris' buddies were enough to draw blood.

Well, she hadn't killed him. Even if she wasn't sorry he was dead. Guilt did surface right then. Loren felt her face flame with a blush as she considered her actions.

She was a complete idiot.

Reckless and foolish just didn't seem harsh enough to describe her actions. How could she finally be free from one man and fall into another's bed on the same night?

It took stupid to a new level.

Walking down the hallway, Loren looked in on Toby. Her son was still sleeping and she knew he would be right there 'til tomorrow morning. Well, at least someone was resting. Her body ached with fatigue. But it was the soreness inside her that really bothered her today.

The small discomfort reminded her of exactly where Rourke had been the night before. It was blunt evidence that she didn't have a shred of willpower anymore. The attraction was too deeply rooted inside her to ignore.

Loren hissed under her breath as she turned around. The master bedroom was right in front of her. She hurried past it but the slight scent of its master still drifted across her nose.

There was nothing to do but wait. She'd awoken to an empty bed and a brief note. Well, it wasn't a note. Rourke had left his orders right next to her head.

Loren bristled again but she wasn't foolish enough to disobey the man. She was restricted to the house. Period. That included the porch. But the looks coming in the kitchen windows told her to steer clear of even those limited escapes from the walls of the house.

So, she turned in another circle before heading for the den. Dread followed her as she considered the very real fact that there was going to be more death on the mountain. Murder had joined disease as both tried to claim more victims.

* * * * *

Sean Loren knew how to handle a weapon. Rourke watched the steady motion of the older man's hands as he reassembled the automatic rifle he'd just oiled. No hesitation, not even the slightest tremble to the man's motions. It was all done with whisper-smooth efficiency.

"I didn't kill the bastard." Loren's father lifted blue eyes to look at Rourke before he returned to polishing the rifle in his hands. "Wish I had."

Rourke snorted. Sean Loren lifted a cocky grin to his frustrated face.

"I've wanted to kill that asshole for years. But I wanted to tear him apart with my bare hands. A bullet was too good for him."

"So why didn't you take Chris for a walk when you had the chance?"

Sean tilted his head as he considered Rourke from eyes that were sharp as a razor. "I didn't want my grandson to be ashamed of me. Had to set a good example for the boy, seeing as how his father wasn't going to do the job. But I would have taken care of it if Chris ever came back around my family."

Rourke nodded with understanding. Sometimes a man had to choose between what he wanted and what his family needed. But Rourke believed the man and that left him with one less suspect on his list.

Sean shouldered his rifle and let the weapon rest across his body. His hand was wrapped around the trigger in the perfect position to be used. The position spoke volumes about the man's familiarity with combat. He kept his weapon hot and his body ready. Sean Loren expected trouble and Rourke agreed with him.

"Watch your six."

Sean Loren nodded in response, but raised a finger at Rourke before issuing his own warning.

"I'm planning on watching yours, sir." Sean Loren's face set rock-hard as Rourke lifted an eyebrow at him.

"I ain't worth a kill. But it's mighty hard for a man to prove himself innocent when he's dead. Wouldn't be any too hard to pin that kill on you, Major."

Rourke nodded and turned away. The older man was right. It would take about five minutes of investigation to determine that he had both the motive and the weapon to fire the shot that killed his man.

The murder didn't make sense. Chris had been reasonably well-liked in his unit. The man was pure Ranger, he lived for the next mission. That left Rourke with only Loren on his list of suspects with motive.

Motive she had, but the facts didn't support her guilt entirely either. Maybe if she'd given up her fight and yielded to his pursuit before her husband was dead, she'd have the reason. But she hadn't committed adultery.

Neither had she signed those divorce papers. Rourke considered his house with hard eyes. The need to know was burning a hole in his mind. The idea that someone could remove Loren from his life made that flame burn higher. No one was going to get between them. Loren was staying right were she was 'til he figured out exactly why he was drawn to her so completely.

The sun was setting and Rourke climbed further into the forest. His senses were alive tonight. The rules of the quarantine didn't seem to be keeping his brother away. Rourke could feel Jared as the man approached him.

Propping his shoulders against a tree, Rourke pulled his gun from its holster and checked the chamber. The forest was silent. Rourke raised his head as Jared slipped silently into view. His brother's eyes ran down his body before he returned them to Rourke's face. A small box came sailing through the air. Rourke caught it with his left hand as he tucked his gun back into his holster with his right hand.

Turning the box up to catch the first moonlight of the night, Rourke read the label on it.

"You've got a lousy sense of humor, Jared." Rourke tossed the box of condoms back at his brother.

"I'm dead serious." The box came back to Rourke as he frowned at Jared. So maybe he hadn't considered protection last night. That didn't mean he needed Jared to remind him.

"I remember the intensity, Rourke. I'll be surprised if you remember to use them even after I brought them to you."

Rourke lowered his eyes to the box in question before he stuffed it into his pocket. Jared had a point. His brother's wife had conceived their child when suspicion still clouded their relationship. He and Loren didn't need any more immediate complications.

"There's nothing wrong with my brain, Jared. My memory isn't attached to my genitals."

Jared slowly grinned, and Rourke snorted at the smug expression. Jared's lips continued to rise until he was smiling like a smart-ass.

"You've got it bad, Rourke. Terminal unless I miss my guess."

"Shut up."

Jared shook his head, but clamped his mouth closed. The stress bleeding from his brother stole the humor from him. Extreme emotions could never be completely hidden from each other. Even if their true talent was in tracking, they were psychics.

Ah hell. Rourke cursed again as he felt his brother sifting across his mind. He was strong enough to throw a barrier up but Jared wouldn't tolerate that for long. Suspicion was an evil demon. Right then it was chewing on his thoughts as his brother tried to discover what caused it.

"Leave it alone, Jared."

"I'd rather settle it."

Rourke pushed away from the tree. "I'll deal with Loren."

"Let me probe her mind. She doesn't need to like me." Jared faced off with his brother. "Besides, she can get around to forgiving me later."

Rourke hooked his hands into his belt. The offer was tempting for about three seconds. Probing the mind was brutal on the subject. A single contact had sent Loren into shock the first time. There was no way Rourke would allow a repeat of the incident.

"She's my woman, Jared."

The smile crawled back onto his brother's face as Rourke silently groaned. The words just slipped out. He wasn't sure exactly where they'd come from, only that he meant them.

"Definitely terminal."

* * * * *

She should have been able to fall into an exhausted slumber. Instead Loren found herself lingering over her shower. Her skin was sensitive. She frowned but raised her leg and ran the soap bar along its length before she applied a new razor to the skin. The two day's growth of hair bothered her immensely tonight. She wanted to be smooth.

Raising her opposite leg, she applied the same sharp blade to it. Steam rose from the water as she tossed her thoughts around her head.

No, it didn't make sense. Reason wasn't anywhere to be found, and well, common sense had dissipated the second she'd set eyes on Rourke Campbell. Taking a final rinse under the spray, Loren turned it off and stepped out of the stall.

The night was cool. She should have been cold but she wasn't. Instead, the idea of donning clothing was somewhat unpleasant. She felt free. Raising a brush to her hair, Loren tried to untangle the strands.

At least sunset brought one soothing bit of information. No one had died today. With each day that passed the danger of further infection weakened. In another week, she'd be free to return to her life.

Return? That was humorous. Quite funny, really. She'd never be the same woman she'd been before meeting Rourke Campbell.

But that wasn't a bad thing. Life was about the journey, not the destination. Surviving the last week was a test to her inner strength. She wasn't a prideful person by nature but being tenacious enough to not panic held true rewards for Loren.

She'd become a quitter the day they buried her, not one second sooner.

Grabbing a shirt, she buttoned it the bare amount to cover her breasts. She didn't bother with a bra. She just wanted a cup of coffee. Stepping into her jeans, Loren snapped them closed before wandering down the hallway.

The scent of coffee drifted to her nose making Loren quicken her pace. She was cold now that she'd left the steam-filled bathroom behind her. The promise of something hot made her smile. But the kitchen counter was bare. Topped with white tile, there wasn't a speck on it and no coffeemaker either.

Loren frowned and sniffed the air again. The scent of rich, dark, freshly brewed coffee was thick. She blinked her eyes and looked over the empty countertop again.

But the scent was there. Turning about, Loren considered the smell. She followed it back toward the master bedroom. The house was built in a square, meaning there were two hallways leading back to the bedrooms. A third one ran across the back of the house. The kitchen took up one corner of the front and a living room took up the other.

The master bedroom occupied the entire right-hand back corner. There was a set of stairs that led to a second story but the door leading to those stairs was locked with a computerized lock. There was a set of stairs outside that led to the second story and the Rangers climbed it to use the second floor as a sniper's nest to protect the compound from. It was just another detail that set the house apart from normal life. Loren considered the hallway as her memory offered up a vivid picture of the night before.

Clever, so very clever. Rourke Campbell knew her just a little too well. Loren shook her head. Well, what did she expect? The man was a hunter. He'd taken the coffeemaker into the master suite just to see if she'd follow the trail and take the bait.

Loren laughed. She was going to remember this. The guys at the local firehouse would be hooting with laughter. Shaking her head again, Loren turned back toward the kitchen. She could appreciate the joke but had no intention of becoming the brunt of it. But she still giggled as she enjoyed the playful hint of Rourke's charm. Every now and then he let the hard edge of manhood drop away to show her the little boy lurking inside him.

"It was worth a try." Rourke materialized from the darkness again. Loren shrieked as he wrapped a blanket of some sort around her. She frantically tried to avoid the trapping confinement of the fabric but he was deadly efficient as he bundled her into a tight cocoon.

"Hey! What are you doing?"

Rourke lifted her squirming body off the ground and gave the lower end of the blanket a sharp tug to trap her legs. Only her feet escaped the confinement, but they weren't any use to her with her legs bound together. Rourke settled her body against his chest before he took the few steps between them and the master bedroom doorway.

"If the trap doesn't work, go for the capture."

His voice was deep but playful. Loren felt her lips twitch into a smile before she frowned as he deposited her on his bed. The coffeemaker was gurgling away in the bathroom making the room thick with the aroma of java.

"Cute. Very cute, young man. Now unswaddle me."

He followed her down onto the bed. One large hand was twisted into the blanket to keep it closed. The moonlight spilled over his face giving her a glimpse of a boyish grin.

"Do you surrender?"

"Excuse me?"

"Surrender. Yield." His voice dipped to a low rumble as he nuzzled her ear. "Submit to my authority."

"Like hell!"

"Hmmm…" His teeth nipped her earlobe making her jump. Sensation shot down her neck and into her stomach. Warm lips gently wrapped around the sensitive area and sucked, making her squirm against the blanket's hold.

"Then you're my prisoner."

Her breath escaped in a rush. Loren sucked in a lungful as Rourke's lips began to kiss a trail down her neck. Her skin sprang to life under his mouth as blood rushed into the tissues of her skin to help intensify the sensitivity of her nerve endings. His free hand cupped her head and turned it up to allow his lips to travel down to her collarbone. Heat rushed up her body like a wave. Loren shuddered as he nuzzled the collar of her shirt out of the way.

The confinement of the blanket and his grip combined inside her with wicked results. Her body sprang to keen awareness as her imagination considered just what Rourke might do with his…captive.

"A little overdramatic, don't you think?"

Her voice was shaky. Rourke raised his head to consider her eyes. There were several emotions drifting up from her. He let his own mind relax and merge with hers in a light touch that was more intimate than anything they'd shared the night before. Loren didn't shy away from it. Her eyes widened slightly but she never looked away. Relief surged through him as Rourke smiled down into her eyes. Just being accepted as he was, hit him square in the chest with emotion that he couldn't quite recognize. But it felt amazingly good.

"Law of the jungle. I caught you, I get to feast on you."

This time she shivered. Rourke felt it with his hands as well as his mind. She kicked against the blanket and he tightened his hold.

Her heart was racing. Loren finally listened to the frantic pounding of her body and smiled. Hunger ran rampant between the two of them, only it wasn't the hard pulse that they'd given in to the night before. Instead it was the steady increase in heat that melted her from the inside out. Like a pair of coals, they were heating each other and glowing with the intensity of it.

A quick jerk and Loren rolled away as he snapped that blanket free. She let her shoulders follow the motion he'd begun 'til she rolled free of the constricting fabric and right over the edge of the bed. She landed on her feet and smiled. Rourke Campbell was one of the strongest men she'd ever encountered, but he still knew how to play. That was something that too many people lost sight of as maturity forged them into adults. Lifting her head, she looked across the surface of the bed to find him grinning like a little boy. He lifted his hand and crooked his finger at her.

Her body leapt as she considered exactly what would happen if she went back onto the bed. The ideas were addictive just like the man who inspired them. Her body clenched as she felt her breasts lift with arousal. Her nostrils flared slightly as she caught the hint of male aggressiveness that mingled with the scent of coffee.

That coffee made her body leap again. He'd actually taken the time to lay a trap for her. Maybe it was arrogant but the possessive nature of that action made her passage clench with need.

His body looked relaxed, but like any predator, he'd snap to attention in an instant if he wanted to. Loren stood up as she considered the power contained inside his body. His eyes were razor-sharp as they watched her. Lifting her hands, she slowly worked the buttons of her shirt 'til the garment hung on her shoulders.

The two sides dropped open to catch on her beaded nipples. All hint of playfulness evaporated from his face. In its place rose the harsh angle of aggression she knew lived inside him. Loren studied his mouth as she rolled her shoulders 'til the shirt dropped down her arms. His lips tightened as he rose up onto one hip.

"Come here, Loren." His voice was deep and edged with steel.

Instead, Loren let her fingers play over her jeans button. His teeth appeared as his face tightened even further. Feminine power was strong as it surged through her. She felt her lips lift into a grin as she noticed exactly how much fun she was having.

She'd never associated the word *fun* with lovemaking before. There were a wealth of other emotions whispering along her body but she was also having just plain fun.

And the jeans were making her crazy. The fabric scraped against her ultrasensitive skin making her tug the snap 'til it popped open. A quick pull on the zipper and Loren let the unwanted clothing slip down her legs. Her newly shaved legs felt amazingly smooth as she let the night air flow over them.

Loren watched his eyes travel over her. They were sharp and keen but she stood proudly before him. Her body temperature rose as she noticed the thick bulge pressing against his pants. He was still lying on his side as his eyes traveled back up to her face.

Some of her confidence fled as she faced the raw emotion blazing from those emerald deaths. Playfulness had given way to pure intent. His body left the bed in a sharp move. He gained his feet in a silent motion that sent a chill through her body. He was so completely solid, each moment of his body precise. The way he moved drove home how efficient a hunter he was.

His boots didn't seem to connect with the floor. He was just in front of her. A warm hand cupped her chin as his thumb lightly ran the length of her lips. Sensation shot down her body, raising gooseflesh and drawing her nipples into tighter points. His eyes fastened onto those hard nubs. A second later the tip of his tongue flicked over her left nipple, making her jump. The touch was too hot, searing with intensity that made her belly clench with need.

Her retreat didn't please him. A low rumble came from his chest. His eyes shot straight to her face as he judged her expression. She felt the same brush of his mind against hers but this time the harsh edge of his need made her shift backwards.

But her own need was too great for fear to truly emerge. Loren shifted again but didn't retreat any further. Her body was yearning for his in a primitive fashion. Liquid heat flowed from her passage as she watched the way his eyes dropped to her breasts again. His large hands began a steady movement that had his clothing falling away in scant seconds. Loren hung on his motions as she was rewarded with the sight of his firm shoulders.

"Come here, honey. Touch me like you did last night."

Rourke could feel the warring emotions inside her. It ignited a dangerous reaction in his brain. Need was erupting with painful fullness inside his head. The smell of her sex drifted up, making his penis stand out, stiff and hard.

The scent from her passage made his nostrils flare. The single touch of hand to chest wasn't enough. He needed to be closer to her, inside of her, body and mind. But first Rourke intended to taste her. The hesitation drifting from her emotions made his body tense to capture her.

Loren gasped as he lifted her. He did it so effortlessly. She knew firsthand what kind of upper body strength it took to lift another human being. Rourke pulled her from her feet like a child.

The bed shifted as she felt it under her back. Rourke came across her body in a solid movement that frightened her with its intensity. He was capturing her, securing her body. She felt the aggressive edge of his emotions radiating from his mind straight into hers. It was overpowering, making her shift as she struggled to maintain some measure of control.

"No." His lips were a bare inch from her mouth as he growled the word. He cupped the back of her head before his lips engaged her mouth in a single motion of conquest. He thrust into her mouth and demanded a response.

It was a potent mixture of domination and intimacy. Loren couldn't separate the two. They shifted together like two different colors of light inside a crystal. She lifted her head to taste him. Her body writhed under his as she strove to get closer. Her thighs parted as her body begged for the deepest touch of male to female.

"Not yet, honey. Tonight, I'm going to taste you."

Her head was suddenly free as Rourke cupped both her breasts. His hands held each one and raised the nipples for his tasting. She shivered as he stayed settled between her spread thighs. It was such a controlling position but it made her shiver with need as well.

The moonlight spilled over him as he extended his tongue to lick the top of one nipple. She jerked as the flesh screamed out with the touch a second before his mouth closed over the beaded point. He sucked it strongly into his mouth as his finger gently massaged the globe of her breast.

"Jesus! I wanted to suck these little nipples of yours." It wasn't a lewd comment. Instead his voice was a deep rumble of appreciation that made Loren sign. His mouth homed in on her opposite breast and he trailed light kisses across her chest to treat it to the same attention. Loren lifted her hand to stroke the defined muscles of his arms. Her fingertips became detailed receptors, transmitting each ripple of firm flesh to her brain.

Rourke flicked a nipple again as he sucked the hard nub completely into his mouth. But the scent of heavy arousal rose between them making him release her breast. Tiny sounds of pleasure came from her throat but they weren't enough. He wanted to hear her cry, feel her body twist in response to his touch.

That hot mouth traveled down her belly. Loren felt the muscles clench as he trailed little kisses over her abdomen and across her belly. Her thighs were still spread open. It was a vulnerable position that she shifted against. His dark head rose to look across her body with firm resolve.

"Let me see you, honey."

Moonlight glittered off his eyes before he returned to his kissing. It would be rather simple for him to keep her thighs exactly where he wanted them. But that wasn't what he wanted from her. Loren forced her body to comply as he brushed a soft hand over her mound. Fire shot straight into her core as she whimpered and craved more of his touch.

The trust she yielded pleased the hell out of him. Rourke watched the tiny quiver of her legs as she battled to relax. Taking her would be simple but he wanted a hell of a lot more. More than sex, he wanted her to yield in every manner. What he wanted was complete trust.

His mouth was scorching. Loren listened to her own cry like it belonged to someone else. His lips fastened onto her sex and pulled the delicate tissue into his mouth. Heat flowed directly into her womb as fluids seemed to drench her passage like lava.

"I can't take that!"

"Yes, you can." It was an order this time. Rourke braced his forearms across her thighs before he gently speared the folds of her sex. His tongue flicked over the small bud he'd revealed before he applied his mouth to it.

She bucked beneath him and he sucked harder. His penis throbbed painfully as he listened to the approach of her climax. Rourke forced his own needs aside as he thrust a single finger into her body. She tensed and froze on the edge of a kaleidoscope of sensation before tumbling into her climax. The walls of her passage contracted around his finger making him growl.

Primal pleasure was etched into his face when he rose up. Loren couldn't move beyond the rise and fall of her chest and she didn't want to. She was still spread before him and there was nothing but need driving her.

The thrust of his body was hard and quick. The walls of passage quickly stretched in memory of his last possession. She moaned slightly as her sex sent out another jolt of sensation. His hips drew back and sent his weapon stroking forward to make her gasp as pleasure rushed back up her body and into her center again. She twisted under his movements as another climax threatened to break over her.

"That's right. Let go, honey. Come with me."

His voice was harsh but hypnotic. It all connected to the powerful thrust of his body against hers. They were melting into a single pool of liquid. Pleasure was coating their bodies like molten silver. Loren lifted her eyes as his hands grasped her head. The harsh rasp of his breath hit her lips as his eyes bored into hers. It was a final merging of intimacy. Her body pitched and bucked to send him deeper. Her fingers clawed into his arms as they both fell into a vortex where the only solid thing was each other. There was the deep thrust of his body before his sex jerked and erupted inside her. It was completing and fulfilling and Loren sent her hips pressing harder into his as she tried to deepen the contact.

Intense. His brother had used that word but this just went a hell of a lot further than intense. Rourke rolled over and pulled Loren with him. His body was pulsing as his head swam with a slightly dizzy wave of completion. His arm clenched her damp body close as he refused to be completely separated from her. There was a deep need inside him to clutch her tight. She wiggled as her mind attempted to regain its individual personality. Rourke held to it as he smoothed her body into place against his.

Tomorrow would be soon enough for them to resume their battle to remain aloof from each other. Tonight they were entangled in intimacy and that was exactly where Loren would be staying.

"Go to sleep, Loren. We can argue about what we're doing in the morning."

His ankles trapped hers as she pushed against the solid strength of the arms that bound her to his chest. She couldn't sleep there. Not again. Loren raised her head but dropped it as fatigue wrapped around her. Maybe they'd just worry about it tomorrow…whatever it was.

* * * * *

She was going to get pregnant.

Loren stared at her own horrified face the next morning. She'd dragged her body out of Rourke's bed and headed for a shower. The coffeemaker was still sitting there on the bathroom counter but with a fresh pot on the warming pad.

It was the small box sitting on the white tile countertop that terrorized her. The box of condoms was open but each little foil-sealed package was in it still, every last one of them.

Oh God!

Loren felt her stomach clench as she looked at that stupid box. At least Rourke had thought enough to get the things out. She, on the other hand, hadn't even considered birth control.

"I guess that face tells me you told me the truth about not on the pill."

She yelped and turned to see Rourke striding back into the master bathroom. The single luggage bag that had arrived with her was hanging from his right hand. He set the bag on the counter before he picked up the box of condoms.

"I think these had better be next to the bed from now on."

Loren stared at her bag as Rourke turned and took the box into his bedroom. Her thoughts buzzed through her head at near light speed, but not a whole lot of them were making any sense.

Rourke turned around to see her standing in the center of the bathroom with her bag hugged to her chest. Her reluctance to set that bag down made his temper bloom. Even in the guestroom, she'd been living out of the bag. The thing was fully packed except for when she was bathing. The second she was done, she repacked her gear tightly.

"Unpack that bag and settle in, Loren."

Her eyes snapped open wide as she aimed a furious look at him. Rourke felt his teeth grind together as she pressed her lips into a tight line of refusal.

"Don't push it, honey. I'd be more than happy to prove to you how much you'll enjoy staying in my room."

He hooked his hands into his belt and stared at her. Loren was caught between the urge to laugh and the need to snarl. Of all the Cro-Magnon attitudes!

"Just because we had sex doesn't mean I'm moving into your room."

Rourke nodded softly. He moved toward her on silent feet. Her attitude rubbed his pride making it vital to prove the issue to her. The bathroom mirrors reflected his harsh expression as he stepped up next to her.

The bag went flying onto the counter. Loren gasped at the power his single arm wielded. He wrapped her into an unbreakable hold as his hand captured her head and tipped her face toward his.

Loren felt her knees go weak as she stared into his eyes. They glowed with primitive rage. She'd thrown the gauntlet down and he'd accepted the challenge. Rourke Campbell fully intended to prove the issue.

His mouth collided with hers a second later. He thrust through her lips to deeply penetrate her mouth with his tongue. But it wasn't brutal. Instead the velvet tip of his tongue stroked the length of hers making sensation erupt inside her. He explored her mouth in a deep motion that sent heat pouring toward her belly. Loren clung to his shoulders as he stroked over the delicate surface of her lips.

His staff hardened against her belly, making her tremble. The arm across her back bound her to his length, making sure she felt the rise of his intentions. Her newly washed skin became ultrasensitive to each and every touch.

Rourke smoothed a hand over her back as he caught the scent of her body. That sweet smell of her passage heating and moistening for him. He lifted her from her feet and sat her on the counter as he used his body to spread her thighs to admit his hips between them. In a base and primal way he needed to make her submit. Force her to face their mutual need for each other. He wanted to listen to her whimper with pleasure.

"Oh God...Rourke...don't." Her throat contracted on the rest of her words. She couldn't think beyond the screaming flesh between her legs. Rourke dropped to a knee and captured the small buddle of nerves in his mouth. His tongue flicked over it with firm pressure, making her body jerk.

Her passage clenched with need as a tiny moan escaped her lips. He lapped over her bud before moving along the entire length of her sex. He stopped at the entrance to her body and gently probed the opening. The walls of her passage contracted painfully as she thrust her hips toward his mouth, yearning for a firmer touch, a deeper thrust.

Rourke denied her that. Instead he licked and sucked along the folds of her sex never staying on one spot too long. Loren simply tried to endure as waves of need and pleasure came too close together for her to separate. She writhed on the edge of climax and Rourke held her there with iron control.

Rourke listened to her moan and curse. His body was raging with need. He wanted to ride her, make her beg, but more than anything else he needed her to yield. He would not let her thrust their relationship into the category of casual sex.

He pushed to his feet in a fluid motion that made Loren cry out. She needed to come, was desperate for release from the screaming demands of her body. Her hips pressed toward the hard bulge of his sex and she moaned again as she cradled it in the notch of her thighs. The harsh fabric of his pants didn't yield the hot touch of bare skin that she craved.

"Do you want me, Loren?"

His face was ruthless. Her actions had wounded his pride. Loren took a deep breath as her hips twisted again and need clawed at her.

"Yes, God yes!"

"Then take what you want."

He stepped back, letting the cool air brush her exposed sex. Loren followed him. She jumped off the counter and reached for his fly. He groaned with deep approval as she unfastened his pants. The thick length of his cock fell through the opening as she gently grasped it. Her passage sent another wave of moisture in response to the heavy scent of his sex. The rod pulsed in her hand as she looked into the blazing eyes of her partner.

"Turn around."

Compliance seemed to be the price for her determination to leave the master bedroom. Loren turned as his arm bound her across her middle. He leaned forward 'til her breasts hung free and his hips nestled against her bottom.

"Now spread your feet apart and lift your bottom for me."

Her temper broke through the raging need as she considered the helplessness of the position. Rourke watched her face in the mirror.

"Do it, Loren. I want you to watch me take you."

The idea stole her breath. Loren looked at the full-length mirror and spread her feet. She was completely naked. The tip of his cock appeared between her legs. The ruby head moved along the folds of her sex making her passage scream to be filled. She pushed her bottom up and felt him move into her body.

Rourke didn't ram into her. He wanted to stretch her inch by inch as he watched her face. Her body clasped his, making sweat bead on his brow, but he was fascinated by their reflection. Thrusting home, he listened to her gasp before he set an even pace to their coupling.

Loren still hung on the edge of climax. The hard thrust of his body appeased the needs of her passage but from behind her the little bud of her sex didn't receive enough attention to let her tumble into release. Loren raised her bottom higher as she tried to take his rod deep enough to satisfy her need.

He gently bent her back into their original position. Her bare breasts bounced with each thrust as he gently cupped one of them. His hand traveled down her belly toward her mons as his body began thrusting harder into her from behind.

"I'm going to make you come now, Loren." A single finger found her bud and pressed on it. His hips thrust forward as he rubbed and pressed again. Loren was frozen in place as she felt him thrust and watched his finger rub her sex in the mirror. His breath was a harsh rasp as he thrust and rubbed again. This time she splintered into pieces as her body tumbled into ecstasy.

Rourke lifted her right off her feet and bent her completely forward as he buried his rod in her body. The walls of her passage clenched and grabbed at him as he jerked with release. Her body milked his rod as he held her over his arm to receive his seed.

Loren gasped as her body sagged. Rourke felt his emotions roll as he placed her on her feet. He caught her head and raised her dazed eyes toward his. He gently kissed her mouth before lifting his face from hers.

"Unpack the bag, Loren."

Chapter Ten

"Come on, Toby. Wake up!" Loren knew how to move an unconscious body when she had to, but her son's lanky frame wasn't an easy one to lift. But she had to wake him up. Toby would run himself to exhaustion and sleep for days. Dr. Jasper had warned them both that Toby needed to learn to manage his brainpower. Sleeping for two days straight wasn't good for the body.

"Tobias Loren! On your feet!"

Loren jumped as Rourke used his voice like a whip. He stood in the doorway with his hands on his hips as he eyed her son.

"What?" Toby raised his eyelids in response, making Loren snort.

"Roll out of that rack and on your feet, mister!"

Rourke's voice was solid steel. Toby rolled over and stumbled as he tried to stand up. Loren watched him with a critical eye. But she let her eyes wander over to the man standing in the doorway. Rourke Campbell was watching her son with those razor-sharp eyes too. He stepped further into the room as he noticed how unstable Toby was.

"Tobias Loren, straighten your back."

"Uh…sure."

"Excuse me?"

"I mean, yes sir."

Rourke softened his voice as he stepped closer to inspect Toby's eyes. He grunted as the youth managed to bring his eyes into focus.

"Get yourself a shower, young man."

Toby nodded and looked for the bathroom door as his mind tried to escape from his deep slumber. Loren shook her head in wonder. Rourke was watching her son stumble into the bathroom with true concern. She'd always been a solo parent. Witnessing Rourke step up to the plate without being asked struck her deeply.

This was a man worth binding your life to. The kind of man a girl could dream of telling she was pregnant, instead of dreading what would happen when she got caught by nature's little need to procreate.

Rourke was the kind of man girls dreamed about and most never met. An ache centered right over her heart as she watched him step into the duty of father even though Toby wasn't his child.

Loren turned abruptly away before Rourke aimed his sharp eyes at her. She was drooling over him. Pathetic as it was, it was true. She reached for the sheets on the bed and began pulling them free.

"Leave them for Toby to deal with."

His voice had lost its commanding edge but it was still hardened with a note that said Rourke expected to be obeyed.

"It's a mom thing. We do it all the time."

"Not today. " Rourke caught her hand and pulled her away from the bed. He raised an eyebrow at her as a ragged breath escaped her lungs. The scene in the bathroom was still a little too fresh in her memory.

"It's time to cut the apron strings. Routine will help him manage that brain of his. Trust me on this one, Loren. I know how to deal with a brain that wants to override the body."

The word "psychic" drifted across her memory again. Loren shook her head as Rourke aimed certain eyes at her. The man was completely confident in his methods.

"Well, I guess maybe you're right."

"I am. Toby is reacting with pure instinct to his abilities. He needs to learn control."

Loren struggled with her pride. Rourke wasn't suggesting anything, he was telling her. He intended to step right into the role of instructor and he wanted her to step aside.

"It's not your job."

"Wrong." His face froze into solid stone. "Understand something, Loren, if you are carrying my child, you'd best plan on me being part of your family."

His arm snaked around her waist and pulled her against his solid frame. His mouth crashed onto her in a hard kiss that made her moan. Rourke thrust his tongue into her mouth and boldly traced every inch of her. Tasting and stroking 'til she kissed him back. Abruptly he released her. He adjusted his pants in a blatant motion that made her face flood with color.

"I've got some work to do right now, honey. We'll have to finish this tonight."

* * * * *

Rourke walked away on steady steps. Loren sagged against the hallway. His lips curled back into a smug grin as he felt the thrust of his body against his fly. Damn, he enjoyed the way her little body felt against his.

The primitive urge to spill his seed inside her made him double his pace. He wasn't just tight. He was hot for her. The smell, the taste, the way she moved her bottom when he rode her.

He wanted to chuck that box of condoms back at his brother's face and forget all about birth control. The idea of binding Loren to his life tempted every wise instinct he had.

But first he had to find out who had killed her husband. The threat of having Loren taken away for suspicion of murder burned a hole in his gut. Jared's suggestion was sounding better every time Rourke touched Loren and felt her body shiver in his embrace.

* * * * *

Men were pigs.

Loren punched another sentence into her laptop keyboard and frowned when she read the screen. She was typing so sloppily there were extra letters in almost every word.

She hissed under her breath. This was so stupid. The tension must be getting to her. Loren considered the odds of turning to sex when death was looming over you. There were experts who would agree she was suffering from that.

But that wasn't the truth and she knew it.

One little fact didn't fit that scene. Rourke had captured her body on that beach. She'd responded completely to a stranger. Well, to Rourke.

But Rourke wasn't a normal man. She smiled as she considered him. He drifted into her very soul and she liked it. Loren shook her head but still laughed a little at herself. She prized her independence. Yet, there was something so erotic about the way Rourke touched her very thoughts.

Her nipples actually beaded, making her push her lips into a pout. Just thinking about the man made her body respond. What exactly did psychic mean anyway?

Toby knew.

Loren cast a look at her son's computer as she bit her lip. As tempting as it was, she wouldn't snoop through Rourke's personal information. She was just going to have to muster the courage to ask him outright or live without the answers.

That left her with considering whether or not she really wanted to know. It would certainly be easier to walk away if she refused to learn any more about the man. So far, everything about him made her more interested in holding onto their time together.

Even the scene in the bathroom drew her to Rourke. It shouldn't have. The modern woman in her rebelled but that didn't change how it made her feel. Chris would have stomped off in the face of her childish refusal to unpack.

Rourke looked her right in the eye before bending her to his will. Loren wasn't sure why she'd enjoyed the domination of the encounter, but she had. It had thrilled her to have him capture her in that manner.

She'd been so helpless in his embrace. Somehow, Loren suspected that had been his intention. Her naked, him clothed. The idea that he could have climaxed without granting her the same release. But it was the fact that he'd aroused her first so that she was willing to lift her bottom for him whether or not she gained that ultimate release. She had been so aroused that any contact had been desired.

Loren sighed as her body began to softly pulse with her memories. The level of intensity confounded her. It was sex, yet the little three letter word didn't seem to be large enough to hold the depth of her dealings with Rourke.

Somehow, she had to find the willpower to stop. This need was growing so deep she was going to drown in it.

* * * * *

Loren's bag wasn't in the bathroom. Rourke looked at the gleaming tile tops, searching for any clue that she'd used them. He leaned into the closet but the bag wasn't in sight. Instead she'd cleaned every last fingerprint away.

Opening his mind he searched for her. He could feel her so intensely, the link yielded the location instantly. Rourke felt his teeth grind together as he considered her actions. She was back in the guestroom.

Touching her mind released a wave of awareness throughout his body. Heat traveled over his frame as he felt his skin tighten with arousal. The temptation to simply walk down the hall and join her was telling him to toss the sheets aside.

But that wasn't what he wanted. Rourke wanted to smash the barricade she was trying to build. Flipping the shower on, he kept their minds linked as he pulled his clothing off.

His staff stiffened and rose to attention as he considered how much he'd enjoyed watching her body as he'd taken her. Running a sure hand over his erection, he smiled as he felt Loren jerk out of her slumber.

* * * * *

Loren bolted upright in her bed. She didn't know why. Her breath was ragged as she tried to leave her dream behind. Instead of dissipating, the images of Rourke followed her. Heat covered her body as she felt the sheer enjoyment from his mind. Pleasure spiked into her brain making her belly clench with need.

Her nipples protested against the top she'd worn to bed. Little points stabbed through the soft tee-shirt as Loren gasped as another wave of heat melted into her mind. It was amazing in its intensity. Her body responded as though Rourke was there with her. Instead she felt her hips twitch as pleasure shot into her brain.

It was male pleasure. Loren felt the bite of his arousal as his staff throbbed and demanded attention. She shuddered as she felt that need rage and burn along his erection until it erupted.

A harsh sound came from her as she fell back on the bed. She twisted in frustration as heavy satisfaction drifted into her thoughts from his. Loren kicked the bedding as her body screamed for her to answer his summons.

Oh, it was a summoning. Psychic…well, the mystery was truly ended now. The man's mind was deadly in its precision.

Well, she wasn't going to be lured into his bed. Loren kicked the bedding again as her skin complained about the rough cotton of the sheets. She hated her clothing but forced herself to roll over and ignore the pulsing need carried in her blood.

Psychic pig!

* * * * *

Rourke leaned against the shower wall and growled. His staff throbbed even harder. The physical release he'd forced with his hand wasn't what he wanted. Hunger ate at his mind trying to reduce him to a primitive level. Transform him into an animal that wouldn't care if he dragged his female into his arms. Just as long as he could bury his face in her skin and thrust his body into hers.

Ripping a towel off the rack, he ran it over his body. His teeth were clenched as he stepped into a fresh set of fatigues. Sleep wasn't an option. Rourke considered the night and then left the house on silent feet. He needed to prowl, to keep his body moving 'til his reasoning overrode the flood of need drenching his mind.

The pulse of his staff told him it might take all night.

Chapter Eleven

Morning took forever to arrive. Loren found herself waiting for it, for the excuse to leave her bed. Sleep was filled with images of Rourke, and keeping her eyes open only managed to banish the crystal clear image of the man. Nothing kept her body from pulsing and yearning.

The second the horizon turned pink, Loren gratefully left her bed. The hours of daylight were critical. If anyone else was infected, the disease should show itself today.

Chris' fellow Rangers might not like her, but today they would deal with her. Loren wasn't planning on hiding in the house when their survival was at stake. She had to know and the men patrolling the compound would just have to deal with her.

Rourke Campbell could take his orders and stuff them.

The morning was crisp. Loren tipped her head back to look at the forest. All the trees in Los Angeles were kept nice and trimmed. Nature wasn't allowed to grow freely. Instead it was surrounded by concrete and buildings.

It was really rather amazing to witness the way the trees took over the landscape. The trees had been cleared away from the compound to allow for the helicopters, but they grew thickly around the area, silently promising to take the land back if man was lax in his diligence to keep the ground.

The scorch mark in the center landing zone was still black. The remains of the helicopter were gone, but the dirt was still dark and discolored from the fire. It was humbling to see it. Life could drag on for endless amounts of time when you were tired of it. Just as quickly, it could become the most fleeting of moments when you were watching the sand grains slip through the center of the hourglass.

Was that the reason Rourke affected her so completely? Loren wished she knew. Maybe she was being a fool to stubbornly sleep in a lonely bed when he'd blatantly beckoned her to join him in his. As she looked at the blackened earth again, Loren felt her reason crumbling. In a week, she'd be dead or on her way back home. It was harsh to acknowledge that Cal's death had given them an extra week together. The man could have contaminated someone just an hour before his death.

"Loren."

She didn't jump. Instead Loren set her shoulders before turning to face Rourke. Her thoughts had been so full of the man it just felt right for him to choose that moment to confront her escape from his house.

Fatigue lined his face telling her she wasn't the only victim of her stubborn pride. Loren lifted her chin as he hooked his hands into his belt.

"I told you to stay in the house."

Lifting her shoulder, Loren very precisely looked at the sleeve of her shirt.

"Hmm…I don't see any stripes. Guess that means I'm not your lackey."

He growled and Loren smiled in the face of his male temper. She was pushing her luck. Rourke Campbell was every inch the commander this morning. Green and brown fatigues were coving his body and seemed to make him look even larger. Power radiated from him.

"I'm not going to be your prisoner, Campbell."

"The last time you came out here, someone died."

"I didn't kill him."

"That would be good to know…" Loren jumped around as another voice sailed out of the early morning light. Another huge man stepped firmly toward her as his eyes inspected her. The eyes were emerald green but different from Rourke's. They were a deeper, browner shade of the color yet still as hard to ignore. They cut right into her head. "…for certain."

He stopped in front of her as Loren forced her back ramrod straight. The man had to be related to Rourke, she could feel him reaching into her thoughts as those eyes darkened into forest green.

"I'm Clay, Rourke's little brother."

"Sure you are."

He curled his lips back to show her his teeth and offered her his hand. Loren stared at it like it was a rattlesnake. Jared Campbell hadn't offered to touch her and the fact that this brother was, was completely threatening.

"You don't see the family resemblance?"

"Actually, it was the word little I wasn't buying. You might be younger, but you and little aren't even in the same ballpark. Unless you were sharing some personal information with me."

Clay dropped his hand as a small grin crossed his face. The expression was far from pleasant. Instead it sent a chill down her spine. This man was ruthless.

"Well, I don't need your help, little brother."

Rourke stepped forward to face off with his sibling. Both men lifted their heads as Jared walked out of the forest. His face was set into harsh lines as he joined Clay in his stand against Rourke. "It's time to settle this."

"I'll be the judge of that."

The hard expression on Rourke's face sparked her temper. The man was torn. Half of him wanted to let one of these men probe into her mind. Rourke's attitude hit her with the force of betrayal.

"It's fine with me."

All three men turned surprised looks at her. Loren only had eyes for Rourke.

"But you will do it, Rourke. My mind isn't open for visitors."

Relief crossed his face, making her temper ignite. Loren dropped her voice before her emotions spilled into her words.

"Just remember something, Rourke. Trust is a two-way street. I did not kill my husband. You know, I don't even understand exactly what kind of psychic you are but I know one thing for certain. If my word isn't good enough for you, then don't bother offering me yours. Trust is a first cousin to faith."

Loren swung on her heel but turned back around. "Nice family."

* * * * *

"You've turned into a hard woman, Lavender." Sean Loren clicked his tongue before he lifted his mouth into a smile for his daughter. "Sometimes a man needs to be objective. Even with his girlfriend."

Loren wasn't sure if it was the word objective or girlfriend she disliked more. But she kept her mouth shut because this was still her daddy.

"I grew strong, Dad. Maybe that means I have to be hard sometimes too."

Her dad grunted and nodded his head. "You've got a point."

Loren considered the source of her dilemma. Rourke was still standing in the middle of the compound with his brothers. Their words drifted up, but were too low to understand. Loren propped her feet against the porch railing and very precisely stared at them. Jared simply raised an eyebrow at her. Clay glared at her. She didn't care. Loren forced herself to toss their looks right back at them. If Rourke wanted to toss in with his brothers and use his psychic abilities on her, he knew where to find her.

"That's a fine young man you got yourself there."

"He's not mine, Dad!"

Sean Loren smiled a crooked grin at her temper. He winked at her before shaking a single finger at her.

"You've grown out of your childhood quite nicely, Lavender. Don't go stupid on me now. A little less pride from you and that man would be wrapped around your finger."

She'd cut her finger off first! Loren glared at her father but he smiled that sweet paternal grin at her. Her teeth ground together as Loren felt her temper strain against the leash she had attached it to.

The testosterone fumes were going to kill her for sure!

Tossing her arms into the air, Loren went back into the house. Rourke and his happy family of predators could just come and find her. Flipping her laptop open, she connected to the county online education program. At least her badge requirements didn't ooze overgrown aggressiveness.

Keeping an active paramedic's badge took hundreds of hours of continuing education. At the present moment, Loren was grateful the county had moved to computerized training for many of those classes. Amidst the medical facts and case studies she could ignore her host's sex appeal.

At least temporarily, anyway.

* * * * *

"Don't make a liar out of me, sir."

Rourke froze as Sean Loren's voice drifted around the corner. The older man stepped up onto the porch and gave him a heavy look. The fact that the retired man still addressed him as sir said Loren's father respected him.

"You have a problem with me?"

"Nope. As I said, I'm hoping you won't make a liar out of me."

Rourke considered the older man and the glint of approval that sat in his eyes. Rourke didn't need the man's blessing but it still hit him in the gut with its beauty. Family was the only thing in life that a man truly held. Well, maybe love too. Extending his hand, he grinned when Sean took it.

"I'll try not to let you down."

The words echoed inside his skull as Rourke considered the silence of his home. He had no clue what to do now. His nose twitched as an aroma drifted on the air. Rourke sniffed again and listened to his stomach growl.

The kitchen was lit and smelled like heaven. Rourke peered around a corner just as Loren let out a silvery laugh. Toby was balancing a bowl on his head as the lanky youth made his way toward the dinner table. He grabbed the bowl from his head as he reached it and bowed deeply.

"Thank you. Thank you. I've been balancing bowls since I was three."

"That you have!" Loren took another look at dinner and smiled as she caught the somewhat familiar feeling of Rourke drifting across her mind. She turned to find him poised in the doorframe with a rather silly smile on his face.

"Hey, dinner's on."

Rourke raised an eyebrow and Loren simply smiled. She was too happy to worry about anything tonight. The sun had set and no one else had died. It was time to count some blessings.

"Hope you like Italian."

Loren turned and bent over to open the oven door. Rich aroma drifted out on a wave of heat. It hit him square in the chest.

There were four spots set at the kitchen table. Emotion threatened to drown him. His kitchen had never been host to a family supper. Rourke leaned against the doorjamb almost afraid to move and spoil the image. He didn't want it to dissipate if he made a wrong move.

"You gonna wash up?" Toby peered around the refrigerator door as he reached inside for something.

Loren folded two dishtowels into makeshift potholders before reaching back into the oven.

The invitation to join them was too much. Rourke stepped into the kitchen and felt his face crack into a ridiculous grin. He flipped the faucet on as Loren and Toby finished setting the table. Sean wandered in and began to pass the salad bowl around the table. His table.

But at the moment it was their table.

* * * * *

"Come on, Campbell, lay 'em down."

Loren's face was an iron mask. She was even managing to erect a rather crude wall to keep her mind concealed as well. Nothing he couldn't break through but it kept her emotions from bleeding out.

"I had no idea that card-sharking was a requirement for firefighters."

Loren laughed. Fire station rules said the poker loser did the dishes. She'd done a heap of dishwashing too. Rourke's firm lips twitched slightly as she eyed him over her cards.

Heat bled across her cheeks as she considered that mouth of his. The man could kiss. Her cheeks stung, making her bite her lip. She'd been able to keep dinner on a purely fun level. But with her appetite for food settled, her body was completely willing to remind her of the substance she'd denied it the night before.

Rourke's green eyes sharpened as she felt him brush lightly through her mind. The edge of hunger his thoughts left behind made her nipples tighten. His keen stare homed in on the telltale lifting of her shirt before he let a smug grin lift his lips.

"Call." His hand slapped his hand of cards onto the tabletop in a sharp motion. Loren groaned as she read the cards. The dirty dishes were calling her name.

She let her cards join his as she sighed and pushed her chair back. Toby chuckled gleefully as he continued eating. Rourke's eyes became razor-sharp as he cast a sidelong look at her son.

He moved with fluid grace. Loren didn't hear his feet hit the floor but the man was out of his chair and halfway across the table before she even blinked. He captured her chin in a firm hold before those lips took her mouth with a firm kiss.

Loren gasped and he pushed deeply into her mouth for a moment of deep penetration. His tongue stroked hers in a long movement before he broke the contact and stood up.

"Supper was delicious. I have to see to a few details before we turn in."

Pure promise was written on his face. He turned to face Toby. Loren felt her face explode with heat. He'd kissed her at the table right in front of her son and father. It took barbaric to new levels.

"Tobias, I want you showered and in your rack before I get back. You will keep the same hours as the rest of us from now on."

"I'm not tired."

"Your body is and it's time to learn how to turn your mind off." Rourke stopped in the doorway and pegged Toby with a hard glare. Her son dropped his fork before he swallowed roughly. Rourke raised an eyebrow at the youth.

"Yes...sir?"

"That's correct."

Loren shoved her chair back in outrage. Toby beat her up from the table.

"Dinner was great, Mom! I got to power down my system and hit the shower. Love ya!"

Her son's dishes hit the kitchen counter a second before he cleared the doorframe. Loren hissed. Her father followed Rourke, leaving her to her temper. She actually stomped her foot and yelped as her bare heel hit the tile too hard.

Pig…pig…pig!

It wasn't fair. Mother Nature was a bitch!

Loren flipped the faucet on and began scrubbing the dishes with every ounce of her frustration. Why was that man right so often? There ought to be a law against it. At least she should be able to stop blushing like a prom queen.

But no! Her body responded to Rourke's even when he wasn't trying to seduce her. She just had to look at him. It went beyond the face or hair color. Attraction was in his every move.

The kitchen was gleaming by the time Loren finally ran out of reasons to stay away from the idea of going to bed. Her stomach was twisted into a knot as she tried to decide exactly what her problem was.

Well, Rourke hadn't returned and that was her main concern. Sometimes keeping that man in sight was rather comforting. On the other hand, the man took bold to the extreme. If he was standing in front of her, she just might find herself in his bed before she got around to noticing.

Oh, damn it!

Loren tossed the dishtowels on top of the washing machine and headed for a shower. She felt her anger simmer as she caught sight of Toby already in his bed. Pushing the bedroom door aside, Loren stepped inside. Deep even breathing hit her ears making her shake her head. Her son was out like a light. It was amazing. Rourke knew exactly what he was talking about.

Well, maybe he should. Who better to deal with a genius than a psychic?

Loren stopped abruptly when she made it into her bathroom. She swung around on her heel to stare at the bedroom. Caught up in her thoughts she'd walked right by and not noticed.

The room was bare. Not a single piece of furniture was left. Her jaw actually dropped. Loren shook her head but nothing changed. An odd sound drifted up from the hallway.

Walking back toward the doorway, Loren listened to the house. It was amazingly quiet here. She was used to the city. The senses became finely tuned when all the background noise was removed. The shower was running in the master bedroom.

Loren blushed again.

She groaned as the heat bled across her face. But she just couldn't prevent the smile that lifted her lips next. Rourke Campbell might be an annoying pig but his persistence was certainly heartwarming. No man had ever cared enough to set a trap for her.

Looking over her shoulder, Loren looked at the empty bedroom.

"You're going to be taking a cold shower if you don't get down to my room soon."

His voice was whisper-soft. Loren felt her stomach drop a full inch as she looked at the man leaning against the hallway. Rourke was in the opposite direction of his room. A shiver actually traveled down her back as she looked into his eyes.

He was stalking her now. Water glistened off his skin as Loren let her eyes trace each and every ridge of taut muscle on his chest. He had a pair of green and brown fatigue pants on. That was it. Her stomach twisted again as heat pooled in her belly. His body seemed to radiate aggression tonight. It was like he'd shed his civilized image and she now faced the core of the predator. There was a primitive purpose gleaming from his eyes.

His eyes sank into hers as that shiver passed over every last inch of her skin. Reasons fled from her thoughts. Right now Loren simply wanted. She wanted the solid strength of that bare chest pressed against her. Hunger erupted inside her making her heart rate double as her clothing became stifling.

Rourke felt his body respond to her on the most primitive of levels. The sensation was intense as he considered Loren. He picked out the stain bleeding across her face and curled his lips back in a grin.

She stepped backwards in response. Rourke slowly shook his head. Need was painful tonight. Hesitation on her part made the beast inside him angry. Rourke pushed away from the wall as he closed the distance. She lifted a foot but placed it firmly under her a second later. Rourke felt his nostrils flare. Her courage made her even more enticing.

Loren didn't understand her emotions. Fear spiked in her heart. She gasped and forced her feet to stand in place. She was being overwhelmed. But she wasn't a coward.

Warm hands cupped her jaw as the scent of a male surrounded her. His eyes cut into her very thoughts as Rourke stepped up until only a bare inch separated them.

It was too great a distance. Loren felt a small cry escape her lips as she lifted her hands to touch him. Her fingertips became intensely sensitive as she traced the strength encasing his body.

"Touch me, Loren."

Her hand slid across his chest, and Rourke felt his staff swell violently. Her nipples stabbed through her shirt making him battle against the urge to rip the fabric from her. But he had a stronger need tonight. Rourke needed her to surrender to him.

His mouth captured her, making Loren moan. His lips were firm and determined. He traced the seam of her mouth before one of his hands slipped to the back of her head and tilted it up. His tongue thrust into her mouth as he stepped into contact with her completely. He found her tongue and stroked it with a deep thrust.

Letting his opposite arm drop, he caught her bottom and pressed her toward the swollen proof of his hunger. Her hips actually tipped forward as Loren sent her tongue boldly after his.

Loren felt her body shiver as he pressed against her. She needed that hard body in so many different ways. His staff burned into her belly making her passage ache to be completely filled. It wasn't about sex. It was the need to delve into intimacy on every level that the human body was capable of.

Her breathing was harsh when Rourke lifted his lips from hers. Loren grasped at his shoulders as she tried to lift her body from the ground. She wanted to be captured.

Held in his arms and taken immediately. A deep growl shook his chest as Rourke gripped her hips and fit his between them.

"Right here, Loren?"

"Yes."

Her thighs eagerly opened in invitation. Rourke thrust his body toward hers and felt the heat from her center burn straight through their clothing. His hand was still twisted in her hair. He tipped her face up until their eyes locked.

"Not good enough." Rourke felt his body strain against the leash he held over himself. He could smell the heat on her. A savage need was rising inside him and threatened to crest over the dam he'd built with his pride. A whimper escaped Loren as Rourke rubbed his erection against her belly.

"In my bed or not at all."

He hooked his free hand into the back of her shirt. A sharp jerk and the buttons scattered onto the floor. His body blocked her against the wall. The night air brushed her bare skin only slightly before his chest rubbed against her. The skin to skin contact made her moan deeply as her body frantically tried to absorb the strength of her companion. Loren felt her nipples scream in protest as her bra prevented the most sensitive part of her breasts from reaching him.

His mouth landed on hers and pushed her lips open for his kiss. Rourke controlled her head as he stroked her tongue with the velvet tip of his own. His staff still burned against her body as she twisted under the hard kiss.

Suddenly he was gone. Loren opened her eyes, frantically searching for her mate. Her body lamented the loss of direct contact, but he was still completely connected to her thoughts. They seemed to have joined into one single idea of need.

Rourke stood with clenched fists as she forced her eyes to focus. She found him three paces away watching her as she bit her lower lip to contain her whimper. Rourke offered his hand to her.

"Are you coming to bed, Loren?"

His terms of surrender made her temper rise but her body refused to listen to her pride. His scent drifted between them making her passage clench and ache for the contact he was refusing her. Her hand landed in his before she even thought about it.

Rourke scooped her off her feet a second later. His feet carried her through the dark passageway with out a sound. It was euphoric. Her blood roared through her ears as Loren indulged herself with touching the bare chest she was cradled against.

He didn't put her in his bed. Instead Rourke set her on her feet in front of the king-sized mattress. His fingers were brutally efficient as he stripped her. A deep rumble of pleasure came from his chest as he bared every last inch of her body.

Loren didn't shiver. Instead she stood proudly before his stare. She wanted to see approval in those eyes. Those emeralds inspected her as his hands made short work of his pants.

The moonlight spilling in through the window bathed him. Loren felt her body heat even further as she looked over him. She was keenly aware of how soft her body was compared to his. Her female gender had been created to cushion his harsher male body.

His fingers stroked over her face. Loren trembled as she felt him close the distance between them. She yearned for the contact yet there was still the most basic of hesitations born from her certain knowledge of his superior strength.

"Shhh..." Rourke folded his body around hers. He firmly stroked her back as her skin quivered. It wasn't true fear, simply reaction. The female response fed his primitive urge to dominate.

Tilting her head up, Rourke captured her mouth. He demanded entry as her hands lifted to complement his embrace. Her hands wandered over his chest as she let her tongue mingle with his in a dance of intimacy.

His hands cupped her bottom as his tongue made deep thrusts into her mouth. Loren was poised on the edge of need. That spot where pleasure and pain became the same sensation. Rourke's hands on her bottom made her passage grow even hungrier for his possession.

Those hands gripped and lifted her up as Loren let her thighs fall open. He raised her 'til she was poised just above his hips. Rourke let their kiss end as he turned and sat on the end of the bed. Loren gasped as the tip of his staff nudged the wet folds of her sex. He gently let her body weight impale her.

His huge shoulders shook. Loren shivered as her body filled with his. Climax was imminent as she clutched at the massive shoulders for support. His hand lifted her bottom as she let her knees clasp his hips. He let her slide back down his length as Loren tightened her grip on his shoulders. This time she rose off his staff and he pushed her back down. His rigid length pulsed inside her as Loren rose and fell on him again. She gasped as pleasure tightened into a knot that clenched with each stroke.

His hands grasped her bottom. Rourke growled as he thrust his staff up into her passage with rapid motions. Climax burst through her belly making her cry harshly as Rourke thrust even harder into her. His staff erupted and filled her as his arms bound her to his body.

Rourke rolled her body on to the bed. He was still buried inside her. His fingers gently brushed her hair away from her face as he pulled his staff from her passage.

Loren gasped when he thrust it back inside her. Tiny waves of pleasure were still radiating from the first climax. His hips moved and thrust again making her passage pulse with renewed hunger. Her hips lifted out of pure need for more of his touch.

"That's it, Loren, lift for me," he growled against her neck as his body possessed hers. Deeply and completely, Loren threw herself into the raging current that bound them both. Their bodies flowed in unison until his seed pulsed into her once more.

* * * * *

Loren awoke with a start. Consciousness slammed into her brain. It was like she'd forgotten something important. Instead only darkness met her eyes. Moonlight was sprinkled across the bed. The silvery glow of moonlight showed her the bare mounds of her breasts. Her nipples were soft now, not tightly beaded. Loren felt her eyes open wide as memory impacted her. She tilted her head to find Rourke soundly sleeping just inches from her.

The moonlight bathed his nude body, making her lips form into a little expression of delight. He looked like some Roman god immortalized in marble, the sort of image that inspired poets and feminine fantasies.

The deep rise and fall of his chest made her sigh. He was very much a man. She caught the scent from his skin as she let her eyes wander over his face. Relaxed in slumber, he reminded her of the playful man who had rolled her up in a blanket two nights ago. The dull ache between her thighs caused a shiver to travel across her skin. There was a playful side to him, yet he was, at his center, a hardened man.

Loren looked back across her own body to see her nipples drawing into tight little nubs. Whether or not she liked it, the harsh determination Rourke wielded over her body aroused her. Maybe there was a part of her that needed to be chased. She'd never really given the idea of domination much consideration before.

Loren felt exposed lying there. They were both on their backs as bare as newborns. Heat radiated from Rourke's large body, so she hadn't awakened due to cold. Rourke had one arm up over his head with the hand under his pillow.

Loren indulged herself in another look over his sleeping body. For the moment she didn't have to worry about him catching her. His chest gave way to tight abdominals. His staff lay against his lower belly. Even soft, the weapon was large. Heat returned to her face making her press her lips into a tight line of frustration.

The way her body responded was infuriating. The fact that Rourke was able to feel it made it worse. She needed some space from the stifling confines of his bedroom.

She was already on the edge of the bed. Loren moved her legs so that her knees could bend. She curled her body gently up until she was sitting on the edge of the mattress. Her toes brushed the wood floor.

A solid steel band encircled her waist and jerked her backwards. Loren went tumbling back into the bed in a jumble of limbs. Her hair flipped over her eyes as she was rolled right over Rourke and onto the other side of his body.

"You should have told me you prefer the left side of the bed, honey."

Loren frantically pushed her hair out of her eyes but being able to see didn't help. Rourke had her on her side as he stretched his solid frame out along her back. His legs tangled with hers as his left arm remained around her waist. His right hand appeared and dove under the pillow. The moonlight flickered over a large caliber pistol that Rourke carried over her body. The bed shifted as he tucked the weapon within his reach before turning to bind her body to his chest with that arm. His hand traveled up her torso to lightly cup her breast. The arm under her shifted to pillow her head as his breath hit her neck.

She was absolutely pinned. Loren shifted her legs as she searched for a few inches of separation from the length of his. Those muscular limbs followed and clamped her ankles between them. She wiggled but his hold didn't allow even an inch of room between them. The fingers cupping her breast gently massaged the tender globe, making small ripples of pleasure zip along her nerve endings.

Loren squirmed away from his hips as they nestled right up against her bottom. His sex wasn't soft any longer. The length of his penis was heating and hardening against her bottom. Rourke grunted in her ear as she managed to pull her bottom out of contact with his erection.

His lips appeared along the column of her throat. He pressed a kiss to her skin before gently sucking along her neck. He leaned over her as his mouth nipped toward the spot where her jugular vein pulsed and betrayed her rising heart rate. His lips gently brushed the pulsing vein.

"I could get used to you waking me up." Rourke rose up onto an elbow as he sucked on her neck again. His hips moved back into contact with her bottom. This time he was halfway over her and pushed her hips into the bedding. A small moan escaped her lips as the length of his erection pressed into her bottom. Her passage erupted with heat as she absorbed the hard length of his cock so close to the opening of her body.

Rourke growled as she continued trying to evade him. It bothered him so completely. But he wasn't mad. Instead, Rourke felt the surge of need pour over his senses until nothing mattered but mastering her body. Releasing her breast, he trailed his fingers across her belly until he found the folds of her sex. Her hips twitched as he sent a firm finger into those delicate tissues. Fluid immediately eased his entry making Rourke groan.

Loren gasped, but her lungs didn't seem to be able to draw enough air into her chest. She found her chest rising with little pants as Rourke found the sensitive nub hidden at the top of her sex. The tip of his finger rubbed over it making her hips twitch. Her bottom actually rose to allow his erection access to her body.

"Hmm…feel free to wake me up every hour."

His finger pressed down onto her nub in response. Loren felt the thick slide of fluid inside her passage. She was powerless to prevent her bottom from rising again. Seeking out the penetration her body craved.

Rourke sighed deeply. He dropped another kiss onto her neck before he began to rub her nub with increasing speed. Pleasure spiked into her belly as Loren found her body poised on the edge of release. Rourke didn't grant her the pressure or speed she needed. Instead she writhed on the border of pain as her body begged for release.

"Rourke!"

"Rourke, what?"

His finger never stopped. That thick erection pulsed against the cheeks of her bottom making the hunger acute.

"Please." She whispered the word, passion moved along her bloodstream like a drug, pulling her further into euphoria.

Rourke used his thigh to open hers. Her bottom lifted as he gently began to rub her pleasure nub again. Her passage was thick with moisture. The walls clutched at his cock as he pushed deep inside her. He listened to his own harsh cry as he pulled back and thrust forward again.

Opening his eyes, Rourke stared at the box of condoms sitting on the bedside table. The animal inside him growled as he thrust into her body again. He refused to tolerate even the thinnest of barriers. He didn't want to don a condom...ever. Rourke wanted to bury his body in hers over and over until she milked him dry.

He held her absolutely still. Loren simply clung to the bedding as his body thrust and withdrew. His finger pressed down onto her nub as his body impaled hers. It was harsh and basic, but completely satisfying with the darkest part of the night surrounding them.

Her cry let Rourke succumb to his most basic needs. He lifted her hips and pounded into her body as she cried out in rapture. Her body brutally gripped his member as he shoved it deeply into her. A savage growl rattled from his throat as he pumped his seed as deep into her body as he could.

Sleep immediately tried to reclaim her. Loren felt it pulling her down into its relaxation as Rourke pressed her onto her back. His mouth captured hers in a deep kiss that demanded a response. Her body yielded to his as she clung to the shoulders that loomed over her.

"Leave my bed, Loren, and I will follow you. Don't test me, honey, because I don't give a damn who watches me take you." She shivered slightly and Rourke brushed gentle fingers along her cheek. "My gun is hot—don't reach for it unless I can't do it myself."

She shivered again as Rourke turned her head onto his chest. He sealed her body along his as she tried to regain her thoughts. He pushed into her mind and firmly refused to let her retreat into her private personality.

Rourke cursed softly as her breathing deepened into slumber. He was hard again as his brother's words floated through his memory.

Intense? *Hell*. One word couldn't possibly describe it.

Chapter Twelve

"Tobias, get on your feet and roll out for morning exercise. Shorts, tee-shirt and your running shoes. Be out front in ten."

Rourke was down the hall, in front of Toby's room, but Loren jerked out of her sleep. She was bundled in the bedding like a toddler. She pushed at the comforter but Rourke's face leaned over her a second later.

"Good morning, honey." His hands landed on the comforter. The fabric drew tight, efficiently trapping Loren in the bed. Rourke's eyes inspected her with sharp motions before a smug grin appeared on his face.

His mouth landed on top of hers. His lips were demanding as Loren squirmed against the bedding again. His tongue traced the seam of her closed lips before one hand released the comforter and captured her chin. Rourke used his thumb to pull her jaw open for a deeper kiss. A small groan of defeat escaped her throat as her lips began to respond to the kiss.

"Go back to sleep. You're not up to running today."

"Like hell, I'm not!" Her temper ignited as Rourke simply looked at her with mild amusement. He sat back as Loren aimed a brutal shove at the bedding. "I made it through the Tower, buddy, despite every chauvinist pig that said a woman couldn't keep up."

Loren launched her body up out of the bed and froze as her lower body shrieked with pain. Her teeth slammed together to contain her cry.

Rourke lifted her chin with one of his huge hands. He had his face carefully controlled in an expressionless mask. But his eyes were alight with delight. Loren raised her fist as her temper exploded.

He caught the blow and smirked at her. Rourke sent her a playful wink before he stood up. His hands adjusted his waistband before he reached for something behind him on the dresser. The pistol came back into view before it was tucked into the back of his pants.

"If you want to be useful, you can make breakfast. I've got a heck of an appetite this morning."

Loren almost screamed. She was certain her eyes were going to pop out of her head. Instead she froze as heard Toby came loping into the hallway. Her temper turned into embarrassment as she frantically dove back into the bedding to cover her nude body. Rourke sent the door shut before her son got a single step into the hallway.

Loren launched a pillow at the closed door. Her missile left a great deal to be desired. It hit the wood panel with a slight *woof* before slipping to the floor. Very unsatisfying.

A groan of frustration echoed around the room. Loren punched the bedding a few times before she forced her body to stand up. A small cramp snaked through her abdomen as she walked toward the bathroom. Loren hissed in response.

She had never been sore after sex! Not even on her wedding night. Heat flooded her cheeks as she headed for a shower. What she and Rourke engaged in just wasn't the same kind of sex that she'd had with her late husband.

Rourke surrounded her. He was gleefully ripping down each and every defense she'd ever erected to prevent her body from indulging in its sexual nature.

Loren stuck her head under the shower and sighed. Confusion was her real problem. She was well past the age of needing permission to have a lover. Maybe if it was only the physical act she could be content. Instead emotions were blossoming up inside her with every move Rourke made.

The man was moving right into her life. Actually, he was maneuvering her into his. His civilized exterior camouflaged a core of pure aggression. Rourke Campbell would get what he wanted. He wasn't a man who understood defeat.

That thought scared her right down to her toes. Loren pulled the sheets free from the bed before heading toward the washing machine. The only thing she knew for certain was Rourke wasn't a normal man. Her eyes caught the morning sunlight as it illumined the sentry on duty. Memory reminded her that Rourke even took his pistol to bed with him. Hot. Somehow, she'd managed to not truly think about his sharper edges. But the man slept with a loaded gun and his home was surrounded by armed sentries. It should have bothered her, maybe even frightened her. Loren shook her head. Rourke inspired a whole range of feelings in her but fear wasn't one of them. She was absolutely convinced that he would never physically harm her.

She couldn't seem to control her body. Rourke conquered it with steady determination and it was entirely possible her heart would be his final conquest.

The certainty of their coming separation made that a fate worse than death.

"Are you actually cooking for my brother?"

Clay Campbell was leaning against the countertop and watching her with dark eyes. The man looked like he'd been there for hours. His body was complexly relaxed as he stared at her. Only Loren knew he must have appeared within the last two minutes.

Being prey to Rourke's ability to toy with her was one thing. His family was another. Loren sent her dishtowel zipping toward Clay. She held onto the far end of it. He immediately raised a hand to deflect her attack. A flick of her wrist jerked the towel back and the wet end snapped with a loud pop on his open palm.

Clay snarled at her. Loren tossed her head and turned to completely face him.

"You must have mistaken me for some pushover female who would be impressed with your solider of fortune, wild man image."

"I scare most of them." He raised a single finger at her. "To death."

Loren simply lifted her hands into the air. She knew Clay's type—proud of their harsh edges. They went to great lengths to appear uncivilized.

"But not you?" A dry laugh came from the man as Loren turned her back on him and gave breakfast a stir.

"Sorry to disappoint you. Why don't you go polish your gun and chew on a few bullets?"

He laughed and moved 'til he was leaning on the counter next to her. Loren rolled her eyes as he attempted to stare her down.

"Don't tell me you're dropping in for a little family meal time?"

He grunted before crossing his arms over his chest. His eyes shifted as she looked at the pan she was cooking in.

"I prefer my meat fresh. Nothing tastes as good as a meal you caught with your own hands."

The man actually fingered the large knife strapped to his thigh. But the action wasn't an attempt at intimidation. It was just a light fingering of the weapon's handle. Loren wasn't even sure if Clay noticed he did it. "Tell me something, Clay. If I act like I'm impressed, will you go away?"

Loren watched him curl back his lips in response. She turned the heat off and walked over to check the oven. "I could make an attempt to simper or tremble or something else girlie."

"You look mighty domestic for all of your tough talk."

"It's not tough talk. I just know your kind, and firefighters have to eat too."

"You have no idea what kind of man I am."

Loren turned and folded her own arms across her chest. "Yes I do. You're the kind of man who would rather bleed to death than let a medic prevent it from happening. Your kind will jump out of a moving ambulance if you can and the consequences be damned. You're the kind of man who would consider sitting through a live production of Annie as the worst torture imaginable."

Clay threw his head back and roared with amusement. His shoulders shook as the kitchen filled with the sound of pure male laughter. His eyes were sparkling with humor when he looked back at her. "I like you."

"Now I'm scared of you."

The man pegged her with a penetrating stare that saw far too much.

"Actually, you're not frightened of me in the least."

Clay sobered and Loren watched the laughter fade from his face. "Kind of a pity because I never poach."

Loren lifted her eyebrow in disbelief. Clay just didn't strike her as the sort of man who worried all the much about boundaries. If he wanted something, he'd do his best to bring in his kill.

"At least, not from one of my brothers."

"I'll buy that."

"Good. That will make this a whole lot easier."

Clay's voice dipped dangerously low. Loren raised her head to watch the way his eyes darkened into deepest forest green. She felt the first wave of contact hit her mind even with the distance between them. Pain slashed into her from the assault. Loren forced her feet to stay in place as Clay began closing that distance.

The precision of his mind was mesmerizing. The pain burned deeper with each step as she found her mind being laid open for him to see, each and every detail of who she was, exposed.

A solid wall suddenly blocked Clay out of her mind. Loren frantically drew in deep breaths as her vision became a swirl of colors. Her vision returned to show her Rourke's back as he stood directly in front of her.

"Get away from her, Clay."

Loren stepped back from Rourke. She'd never heard him sound so completely lethal before.

"This affects every man on the mountain, Rourke, not just your unit. The fact that she's your woman makes it necessary to make certain."

"The only thing you have right, Clay, is the fact that Loren belongs to me." Rourke advanced on his brother as his body drew as taut as a bow. Rage made his movements sharp. "And I don't share."

"You share this mountain." Jared Campbell was as deadly serious as both his siblings. He appeared in the doorway as Rourke turned to keep both men in his sights.

Having Rourke overwhelm her was one thing. Loren found herself unprepared to deal with him protecting her. It produced tender emotions that made her consider deeper feelings.

Instead she faced off with his brothers. "So, are you guys saying that every man serving on your mountain believes in your psychic abilities completely?"

Jared Campbell shifted his sharp eyes to inspect her face. "What exactly do you mean by that?"

Loren shrugged her shoulders as she caught Rourke and Clay watching her as well. "Just wondering if you are really interested in this mind thing for yourselves. What the three of you say isn't worth much if your men don't believe in the paranormal."

Rourke's brothers grunted, but Loren wasn't interested in their response. Her eyes were glued to Rourke as his eyes considered her. She felt the very distinct brush of his mind across hers but it wasn't painful. Instead Loren simply relaxed as the sensation was familiar. Her memory was rich with remembered pain but this was Rourke and Loren knew that he wouldn't hurt her.

She didn't resist. Rourke looked into light green eyes that allowed him complete access to her thoughts. He could have forced the link despite any resistance from her but Loren was yielding it. Trust. That word surfaced between them as Rourke slowly grinned.

"I told you two, no one is going to probe Loren for anything." Rourke turned to look at Jared. "Be a pal and take Clay for a walk. You remember how it is when you need a little privacy."

It was a completely public statement of ownership. Loren felt the heat bleed into her checks but her temper never showed up. Jared Campbell inspected her face before the man very deliberately grinned at her.

"Yeah, I know what you mean, Rourke."

"Well, I don't." Clay glared at her over Rourke's shoulders. It was highly evident from the man's face that he wasn't happy with the change in plans. "A woman is a woman, they all have the same parts. One or another, it doesn't matter."

Loren laughed. All three men looked at her like she'd lost her mind. She leaned all the way back onto the counter to look at Clay. "Spoken like a true savage. Maybe you should apply to be an astronaut. That way you could go land on a primitive planet and make yourself at home."

"There're plenty of women that like me right here on Earth. You just can't see them through those rose-colored glasses."

"I like my rosy shades. In fact, I slip them on every time I get off duty and can leave the ugly side of reality behind me." Loren decided to be finished with the entire thing. She pushed away from the counter and walked right around Rourke. Clay Campbell immediately abandoned his lazy stance as she faced off with him.

"Bring on whatever you got or get out of my face."

Rourke's fingers curled around her biceps and Loren took a moment to glare at him. His eyes clashed with hers before she very pointedly gave her attention back to Clay.

The corner of Clay's mouth lifted. His eyes bored into her skull, making her head ache, but Loren forced her body to stand in place. He didn't push into her mind though. Instead he considered her blatant willingness to endure his mental probing.

"Maybe I should reconsider my position on poaching."

Jared laughed from the doorway as Clay sent her a grin. Loren rolled her eyes as she propped her hands onto her hips. A rather wicked smile lifted her mouth as she looked back at Clay.

"If fate has any sense of justice, you'll fall in love with an Amish preacher's daughter."

* * * * *

"You need a nap."

Loren jumped. Her thighs hit the low table she was using as a desk in Rourke's office. Her lightweight laptop computer went sliding across the smooth surface of the wood making her frantically grab for the thing before it went crashing onto the floor.

"I'm fine."

"Actually, Mom, you look like death warmed over." Toby looked up at her from his nest of computer cables and printouts.

"Gee, thanks." Toby tossed her a smile before turning back to his work. Loren shook her head before she tried to replace her laptop in its rather precarious position.

A large hand landed on the top of the unit and snapped it closed. The computer instantly shut itself down.

Her chair went skidding back from a well-placed kick. Loren raised her head to have her wrist captured and yanked. Her body went tumbling forward. Rourke bent and caught her over his shoulder. He pushed himself up onto his powerful legs in half a second.

"Put me down!"

He did. Right in the center of his bed. Loren bounced on the thick mattress and flipped her body up to glare at Rourke. A wave of pain choose that moment to snake through her skull. She'd been fighting the headache all day. Clearly, bouncing wasn't something that mixed with migraines very well.

Two warm hands appeared on either side of her head. Rourke's fingers gently tipped her face up as he leaned in to consider her eyes. He was on his haunches between her knees on the bed as he brought his face eye level with hers. His mind brushed against hers in the lightest of contacts. Another wave of pain attempted to split her brain in half.

"Clay is too blunt."

"Meaning what?" Loren was way past caring what questions might be best left unasked. If Rourke was going to play around in her head, she had a right to know what kind of psychic he was. The consequences could go straight to hell. It was her head after all.

Rourke rubbed her temples again as her green eyes aimed their question at him. The temptation to just answer her was thick. It would be so damn easy to share the part of himself that he'd never been able to expose to anyone outside his own family.

Loren's face was the same shade as new snow. Dark circles ringed her eyes. Pain had carved deep lines around her mouth as she stubbornly refused to fold under the strain. Her strength hit him right in the gut. A hot wave of lust actually swept through him as he considered how much strength there was wrapped up inside her body. It enhanced her appeal to him in a manner that civilization could not explain. All he wanted to do was roll her onto her back and mate with her 'til her belly swelled up with his child.

Primitive, harsh, Rourke didn't really care. He'd spent his entire life delving into the human mind. Emotions rarely made sense. Honesty lived in a person's truest feeling. You couldn't disguise them.

Loren was only wearing the thin pair of running shorts again. Lust sank its fangs into him as the scent of her sex drifted up to his nose. The heat rose inside him 'til Rourke wasn't certain if there was anything that mattered more than connecting with the sweet female flesh in front of him.

Her eyes widened as lust raced through their link. A deep breath shuddered out of her chest as the tip of her tongue appeared between her lips. Watching her lick across that lower lip was too tempting. Rourke tightened his hold on her head and leaned forward to capture her mouth with his.

It was simply right. Loren gasped and opened her mouth for him. His taste swirled around her mouth as his desire floated on a thick wave into her mind. It was the most erotic experience of her life. Her body sprang to life as intimacy began in her thoughts first. Loren felt his need pulsing through her brain as her body protested the distance between them. She sent her hands to tug on his shirt. Little sounds of frustration hit her ears as the green and brown fatigue shirt resisted her efforts to reach his bare skin.

Rourke pulled their lips apart as Loren moaned. He stood up and made short work of his clothing. His body needed freedom. The clothing infuriated him when his nostrils could clearly smell the scent of Loren's heat.

Loren actually purred with satisfaction as she laid her hands on his newly bared chest. The amazing strength of his body made her mutter with satisfaction. She traced the ridge of muscles before leaning forward to inhale his male scent. Need coursed through her bloodstream as she filled her lungs with his heat. Her fingers found a flat male nipple. Loren smiled as she rolled the tip between her fingers. She raised herself onto her toes to catch the nipple between her lips.

Rourke cupped the back of her head as he growled lightly. Loren sucked the nub into her mouth before sending her tongue to flick over its peak. She was mad for the taste of him. He filled her mind and she desperately needed their flesh to be joined just as tightly.

The metal sound of his zipper being lowered hit her ears. Loren opened her eyes to watch his male organ fall into view. Looking at his bare staff wasn't lewd, she simply needed to see the proof of his desire in the basest manner. His staff was stiff and swollen as Rourke pushed his pants down his legs. Loren endured the separation from his body as he stepped out of the garment.

They'd never made love in full light before. Loren decided she'd been cheating herself. No matter how amazing his body looked bathed in moonlight, the afternoon light was far superior. Her eyes traveled down his chest to the blunt thrust of his sex. On impulse, Loren reached for it and curled her fingers around its length.

A harsh breath caught in his throat making her bolder. Loren slipped her hand up toward the head of his weapon as her confidence grew. Rourke's hands were clenched into fists as she caught the head in her palm and moved her hand back down his length. The veins on his forearms stood out as she worked her hand up and over the head again. Self-confidence surged through her, but more importantly, Loren smiled as she felt to the pure enjoyment coming from Rourke's mind.

That pleasure empowered her. Loren slipped to her knees and gently sent her tongue toward his staff. His hands tangled in her hair as she experimented with her technique. Having him inside her mind let her share the hot surge of pleasure that resulted from her actions.

His breath caught as Loren clearly felt the edge of his control dissipating. She rose slightly and captured the head of his sex completely in her mouth. Loren let her tongue move around its width as her fingers stroked the length. His fingers clutched at her hair as his hips jerked.

"Loren...stop..."

She didn't and Loren considered the pleasure erupting through their joined minds. Rourke was past the ability to think. Pleasure crested over his body as she increased her attention to his sex. His hips jerked forward as he began to empty his seed into her mouth. Pleasure burst into her mind in pure streams of sensation.

"Dear Christ, Loren."

Rourke plucked her off her knees like she was a child. Her tee-shirt went right over her head before he clasped her tightly to his chest. His lips gently nipped the spot where her neck connected with her body, making pleasure erupt from the spot. Loren let a delighted purr come out of her mouth.

Her back was placed gently onto the bed before Rourke came down beside her. His eyes were still glazed with pleasure making her grin.

"I never realized the paranormal abilities could have such personal benefits."

"Loren, do you know what it means to know too much?"

The serious note in his voice bothered her. Loren watched his face set into a deep frown. She reached for the side of his face and let her fingers stroke the warm skin there. Loren forced her mind to stay open as she refused to lose the intimacy they were sharing.

"The only thing I know for certain is that I don't want to think beyond what I feel at this moment. Make love with me, Rourke."

Listening to her own need made Loren shiver. She'd completely bared her soul to him and the seconds that crawled by as he inspected her with his eyes made her tremble with fear. The truest form of that emotion filtered across her mind as she considered being rejected. Sex wouldn't be enough. She needed him to stay joined with her thoughts as pleasure spiked through her flesh. Experiencing it from his mind had been too joyful for her to accept anything less.

Her words hit Rourke with lethal force. Intimacy was a word that he'd never actually understood the meaning of 'til that moment. Her need bled through his mind as he absorbed the desire burning along every inch of her body. It all mixed into a combination that was explosive. He caught the side of her face as he lowered his head 'til mere millimeters separated their lips. Their breath mingled as he watched the pupils of her eyes dilate with pleasure.

"I thought you would never ask, honey."

His kiss wasn't hard. Instead it was deep. Loren let her mouth match his as his tongue thrust toward hers. He stroked the length of her tongue, making her moan as desire gripped her body. She needed so many things in that moment. Loren twisted toward his body as her skin demanded to be touched.

Rourke pressed her back. His hands captured a breast as he sent his lips down the column of her throat. Loren lifted her chin to present him with more of the sensitive skin. His lips were hot as they licked and nibbled down toward her shoulders. One hand found his back as he leaned over her body. Loren eagerly sent her fingers threading through the crisp hair that covered his skin.

Warm lips closed over the peak of her breast through the fabric of her bra. Loren arched her back to offer it to him. Rourke rewarded her with a deepening of contact. The velvet tip of his tongue rubbed across her nipple. Waves of pleasure traveled across her body until they reached her belly. A firm hand smoothed across her skin along the same path. His hand settled onto her belly as his lips moved to her opposite breast.

Rourke listened to the tiny sounds of pleasure coming from Loren. Linked together with her thoughts, he felt desire riding him as harshly as it had when he'd carried her into the room. The scent from her deepest center filled his nostrils as he applied his tongue to her nipple.

Rourke stripped her shorts down her legs. Loren giggled as he rose up onto one elbow and tossed them across the room. A playful grin appeared as she fingered the strap of her bra.

What's your hurry?"

Rourke raised an eyebrow in response. Playfulness mixed with the heavy scent of desire as Loren smiled at his impatience.

"No hurry at all, honey. In fact, I think I might be able to outlast you."

He landed between her thighs, making Loren gasp. His eyes promised pure devilment as he pushed her legs up over his shoulders. His fingers gently pulled the folds of her sex open before he lowered his head to taste her.

Loren's fingers dug into the bedding. Pleasure hit her as his mouth was drawn to the exact motion she craved. Sweat beaded her face as she twisted and bucked beneath his attention. Climax broke over her body three times before he raised his eyes to hers.

Loren couldn't move. Her body was a slave to his. He rose over her in a fluid motion that made her stop breathing altogether. Pleasure radiated through her body but she yearned for the completion of their mating. His eyes glittered with deadly intention as he settled between her thighs.

His penetration wasn't hard. Instead it was solid and steady and deep. Incredibly deep. Loren grasped his hips as she raised her own to complement his thrusts. His eyes bored into hers as his mind sank as deeply as his body. They weren't two genders in that moment. Instead they merged into a single entity that breathed together and felt as one.

Chapter Thirteen

The forest was stunning at night. Loren smiled as she filled her lungs with the fresh air. Call her romantic, but the clean, fresh scent of forest made her giddy. She hadn't stepped foot outside the Los Angeles county limits in four years.

Absolute serenity surrounded her. Well, it was more than that. She was tangled in a net of emotions. Only she didn't feel trapped. The only thing that bothered her was the approach of the end of their quarantine.

Ebola Tai Forest had a seven to ten day incubation. Cal Worth had died after four days. The odds were high that the man was the sole carrier of the disease.

That left Loren to face the fact that she'd be returning to her life at the end of the week. She should have kept smiling. Instead, the expression melted off her face.

She needed to leave Rourke. This mountain, for all of its simplicity, hid a secret that was huge. If she didn't get off the tree-studded landscape, it was going to close around her and trap her behind its mirage of camouflage.

Loren had never thought outside of science fiction movies about psychics. Now, she'd run straight into the reality of them. The heavy presence of special operation military personal told her to squeeze her eyes shut before she saw something else.

Loren wasn't a fool. Her father was one of these people. Bits and pieces of odd information she'd heard from her father confirmed just how serious the military took its secrets.

Men like Rourke never left the service. Civilians like her never really found out that they existed.

And now she knew. Her smile returned as Loren considered the way Rourke merged with her thoughts. It was so completely intimate. Maybe some women might find it frightening. Loren found herself craving it, him, them.

"You're so pretty."

Loren froze. The words were deeply hollow. In the dark, the black-skinned Ranger was almost invisible. His hand reached forward to finger some of her hair.

"So very soft." Moonlight flashed off the gun in his opposite hand. Her stomach knotted as she considered the possibility of Chris reaching beyond the grave to exact his revenge on her.

But the weapon didn't level out in her direction. Instead the solider stepped even closer to her back and stroked his hand over her neck. Loren didn't move. A man like this didn't need a gun to kill her. He could snap her neck with a single hand.

Instead he sniffed her hair.

"Yeah…women are so good-smelling. I should have married one. Chris should have gone home to you instead of letting Cal talk us into those sluts. A whore doesn't smell pretty like you do."

Loren surged away from the man. She was desperate to get away from him. Her nostrils flared as the metallic scent of blood wrapped around them.

"Hey, now, I just want to touch your clean skin. Won't hurt none."

The gun dropped from his hand as he secured her to his body with those large arms. His body pressed along her back as Loren struggled against panic. The man was out of his mind. The horrible smell of fresh blood hit her senses as he began to pet her arm next. She couldn't see in the dark but the forest air blew against the fluid his hand left behind on her skin.

"Steven, let the lady loose now."

Rourke's voice was calm. But he wasn't anything close to meek. Rourke clamped his control into place as he tried to talk his Ranger into releasing Loren. When a man was dying he often sought out a female. It was genetically coded into their brains.

"I ain't hurting her none, sir. She just smells so sweet. Not like a whore. Last woman I held was a slut, a murdering, dirty whore that spread her poison all over me. And I paid her to kill me."

He sniffed her hair again as Loren gently tried to wriggle away from his embrace. She was terrified of moving too much. If she pressed against him, her clothing wouldn't protect her from his infected blood. The man reeked of fresh blood just like a trauma victim did when Loren was transporting them.

"Hey now, be nice, Steven don't hurt pretty girls like you." He stroked her neck as he forced her body back into his embrace. "See…I don't plan on dying like a coward. Your husband begged for that bullet like a baby. I got sick of listening to him whine."

"Hey, Steven, I've got a ten-year-old scotch in the cupboard. Want to join me in a nip?"

His man turned in a slow and eerie manner. He simply let go of Loren before turning to face him. Rourke looked at the harsh reality of the disease. Steven Nelson's eyes were sunken back into his head as his skin glistened with his blood. Loren silently rolled her body over the porch railing. Rourke listened to the soft sound her boots made as she landed on the ground. Fear coursed through him in a solid wave as he considered Steven again.

Someone nudged his elbow and Rourke turned to find his sergeant with a bottle of scotch in hand. Three glasses were tucked under the man's arm. Rourke poured out the liquid before handing one off to Steven. There was a code shared between men who braved combat together. Dying with dignity was one part of that. The rest of his unit looked through the latticework on the porch railing as Steven's breath became a hollow rattle in his chest. Steven raised his glass to the men of his team before tossing it back.

"Right decent of you, sir. I told Chris he was a baby. Asking for a bullet when he could have died with a good drink in his hand. I ain't sorry I shot him." Steven reached into his vest pocket and pulled an envelope from it. The crisp paper turned crimson around his fingertips as he held it toward Rourke.

"You understand me, Campbell? It's all here, signed and dated. I got to break my word to my buddy, 'cause I can't be facing God with this on my conscience. The Lord wouldn't be too forgiving if I let someone take the fall for my killing." He looked confused as he searched the porch beneath his feet. He dipped down to grasp the handgun he'd held in his hand but couldn't seem to find the strength to stand back up. The man landed on his backside as he frowned up at Rourke. He lifted the gun toward his commanding officer, handle first.

"Round is still in the chamber."

Rourke never reached for the weapon. Steven fell back unable to hold up his body. He was dead before his back hit the deck.

Rourke jumped over the body and his railing in one motion. Loren stood facing down his men. His unit medic was inching toward her determined stance as Rourke landed in front of her. His man stopped and raised an eyebrow at his commander.

"Sir, permission to break conduct code? She won't let me touch her."

He wasn't really asking. The man already had his hands covered with thin latex gloves. He'd sat his main weapon aside as he prepared to tangle with Loren.

"Stay away from me."

Her voice was whisper-thin. Rourke used his body to cage her between himself and his medic. He felt the blood freeze in his veins as his eyes adjusted to the meager light on the front driveway.

Against Loren's fair skin, Steven's blood stood out with nightmarish effect. She held her hands away from her body as she tried to deal with the situation. She snapped her eyes into sharp focus.

"I mean it, Campbell!"

"So do I, Loren."

He pushed straight into her mind with his determination. Loren actually wavered as her sight went black momentarily. She sucked in a deep breath as she fought to stay on her feet. She would not place Rourke at risk as well. Every cell in her body rebelled against the idea of harming him.

His head jerked up as her emotions bled across their link. Loren looked into eyes that battled against her mental needs and the need to physically aid her.

"Get some gloves on, Campbell."

A hard nod was her only concession from Rourke as Loren watched him pull the latex protection over his hands. There wasn't a single force on the planet that would stop him from dealing with her himself. She might lament that fact but it was who he was.

But she needed help. Blood was smeared up her arms and across her face. A few fingers were contaminated as well. She didn't dare try to even unbutton her shirt. A sharp edge on a button could cut deeply enough to let the disease into her body. The less she moved the safer it was.

But she had to get out of her clothing before the blood that was on the fabric seeped through the fibers to yet more of her bare skin. She needed help but it would place anyone that offered assistance at risk.

Rourke's eyes moved over her in sharp assessment. Loren recognized the professionally trained way he began to separate their personal relationship from the treatment her body needed. Loren knew it because she'd performed the action herself.

He reached for a knife that was strapped to his hip. The blade flashed as he pulled it free. The sound of separating Velcro told her Rourke's man was in agreement on just how to get her clothing off her body. Only Rangers would have felt so confident about using a blade under the circumstances. Loren clenched her teeth together as she steeled herself to allow them to strip her.

"Stand absolutely still, Loren. Don't even breathe."

Instead she cringed as she felt him place himself in harm's way for her. Loren would have rather died.

* * * * *

"Mom, are you okay?"

Loren lifted her chin to smile at her son. Two hours later she was as all right as she could be. Her body was also clean enough to eat off.

"Sure am, buddy. Better now that you're here."

"Cool. So, like, am I leaving or staying?"

Loren felt her eyebrows draw together. The front door opened to admit Clay Campbell. His eyes immediately scanned her from head to toe before he aimed them at Toby.

"Evening, roommate."

"Excuse me? Is my son going on safari with you?"

Clay grinned at her before he sent a whistle through the house. He grinned at her as he fingered his knife again. "I thought we'd go hunt tigers and chase snakes through the brush. Maybe sleep out in the rain in nothing but our shorts. You know, guy stuff."

Rourke appeared with hair that still glistened with water and his feet were bare. The shirt he wore was marked with dark patches from where he shrugged into it without toweling off first.

"Don't worry, Mom, I'll make sure he keeps out of classified files too." Clay winked at her before smiling at Toby.

Toby swallowed roughly in response. Clay tossed his head back and laughed. Loren met Rourke's eyes and smiled. He was right. Now that the mystery of infection was uncovered, and laid completely on Rourke's men, there was every reason to get Toby out of any possible threat. Her son had had extremely limited contact with Rourke's unit.

But if Toby stuck around it was going to be a chore to remember to keep him at arm's length. The stakes were too high to leave it to chance.

Besides, if she did contract Tai Forest, the last thing Loren needed was to have her son witness the ordeal.

"Take your grandfather along. It's been a long time since he took you fishing."

"Fishing, Mom?"

Loren smiled. If it didn't have a circuit in it, Toby wasn't interested.

"I just might have another Panther at my place."

A grin appeared on Toby's face before he loped into the den and reappeared with his duffel bag and laptop. He tossed her another smile before eagerly following Clay out the door. With the confidence of immortality that youth provided, Toby never looked back.

* * * * *

She looked so damn normal. Rourke felt his jaw clench tight enough to crack his teeth. Right then, tiny microbes could be speeding through her veins intent on destroying her body. They would break down the cell membranes 'til the very fibers of her flesh failed to hold her own blood.

She lifted her head, making Rourke snap his mind closed. He reached for her anytime he was thinking about her. It was almost a form of greeting between them. The thing that surprised him the most was the fact that Loren didn't seem concerned about it.

She accepted him for what he was and it hit him with the force of a chest kick. He'd failed to secure her. Rourke felt his lapse of judgment hit him even harder. The penalty was much too high.

"Will that letter be enough to settle your men?"

"Don't."

His voice was harsh. Loren set her mug aside as she glared at him. She wasn't in the mood to be bullied. His mind snapped back into contact with hers before Rourke stepped forward to close the distance between them.

"Don't you dare begin cleaning up the details, Loren."

Her temper died silently as Loren watched him move even closer. Terror snaked through her thoughts as she recognized the familiar feel of his desire brushing her mind.

"You can't touch me, Rourke." He kept coming as she scrambled up onto the kitchen counter. "Please stop."

"I'm not even sure death could prevent me from touching you, honey."

His strong hands closed over her cheeks before sliding down her neck. A low moan rose out of her throat as Loren fell against his chest. She needed him so much. The smell of his skin, the sound of his heart beating inside that powerful chest. She just needed to be pressed to him in the deepest embrace 'til nothing mattered but each other.

A tiny sob escaped her as she realized Rourke refused to let her protect him. His hand cupped her chin and raised it to meet his mouth. His lips were solid and demanding. He pushed her mouth open as his kiss became deeply intimate.

Loren clung to him. Nothing stood in her way. She was simply free to indulge in her desire. The warm scent of male surrounded her as she sent her fingers toward the buttons on his shirtfront.

He pulled his head up and looked out the window behind her head. Loren didn't blush. She didn't care who might catch a glimpse of them. In fact, she didn't care if anyone decided to watch. Just one short day ago, Rourke had threatened her with that, now she didn't care who knew she was his lover.

Rourke grinned as he caught the drift of her thoughts. Boyish glee sparkled in his eyes even as she saw the shimmer of something harder cross his face. He stepped back as he memorized her face. One hard muscular arm rose toward her. Rourke turned his palm up and offered it to her.

"Let's go to bed, honey."

She laid her hand on top of his. The beast inside him surged with victory. Rourke turned and let his lips curl back to show his teeth as she followed him. Nothing he'd ever accomplished had ever pleased him so much.

The house was completely dark. Rourke left it that way. Tonight he simply wanted to immerse himself in the feel of her flesh, the feminine scent that radiated from her skin when desire made her blood heat for him. His cock tightened with need as he walked through the doorway of his room.

He ripped her shirt off again. Loren giggled as she listened to the buttons hitting the floor. The aggressive approach to baring her body was the deepest of compliments.

The harsh sound of his zipper lowering made her smile. His shape bent in the dark as the sound of fabric being pushed around hit her ears. Rourke straightened before her. She felt the firm invasion of her thoughts as he joined them together before reaching for her.

Her skin rejoiced as they collided. Her breasts lifted as the nipples drew into tight peaks against the rough hair of his chest. Heat fell like a waterfall into her belly. She could not wait even another second for complete intimacy.

Rourke sucked his breath in as her desire burned him. The intensity of that need dissolved every last dictate that society held over him. The rules of modern lovemaking didn't mean a thing. He wanted to impale her body and nothing mattered but thrusting into the hot passage that he could smell. His hand pulled on the lace edge of her panties and pulled the garment off her body.

His hands caught her bottom as Loren sighed with pleasure. Rourke was burned so deeply into her mind that her body was envious to join. He turned and lifted her. The wall touched her back as he kept moving forward until her thighs parted for his hips.

"Wrap your legs around me."

Loren lifted her thighs high and he moved closer to her center. The folds of her sex parted as she wrapped her legs around him. The hard tip of his cock probed her body as she tipped her hips toward him.

His thrust was hard. Loren clung to his shoulders as his body shook with the effort of controlling his thrusts. A primitive urge to mate raced across their link to enflame her body even more.

"Yes, Rourke, exactly like that. Take me."

His eyes flashed at her before his fingers curled into the cheeks of her bottom. Loren let her thoughts fall away as he rammed his hard erection into her body. He bucked and thrust with hard driving force as she clung to him. Pleasure shot out from the friction as she sent her hips forward for even deeper contact.

Climax refused to wait. It cascaded over her in a deluge of sensation as her mate rammed solidly into her spread body. It was harsh and hard and her body gleefully gripped his staff as she felt him erupt inside her passage. Her very womb was reaching for his seed as Loren felt the muscles of her sex milking his staff.

His huge shoulders shuddered as his hand tried to rub her bottom to relieve the sting of his harsh grip.

"Dear God, Loren...I didn't mean to be so hard."

This time she tipped his chin up. Loren stretched forward until their lips met. He let her lead the kiss. The tip of her tongue gently traced the firm outline of his mouth before she sent it into his. He turned with her body still wrapped around his and walked toward the bed. Loren let her legs relax as the mattress took both their weight.

Rourke rolled 'til he rose up alongside her body. He pressed her onto her back and smiled as the silvery moonlight illuminated her body for him. A hundred different places on her skin begged for close inspection. Rourke was going to spend the rest of the night finding each and every last one of them.

"Now, let's make love."

* * * * *

The morning was cold. Loren smiled as her cheeks stung. She wrapped her fingers around her coffee mug and stepped out further onto the porch. Half of it was missing.

She stared at the edge of planking that had just been cut away from the house. The dirt was lifeless because it hadn't seen sunlight in years. The Rangers had cut the porch away and burned it with their fallen comrade.

She turned to lean over the opposite railing. Two sentries walked by with their rifles sitting confidently in their grip. Their eyes moved over her as they considered everything that surrounded them. Loren was used to it now. The mountain home was very similar to a military base. Patrols moved constantly over the grounds. The only privacy available was inside the house itself. The Rangers didn't enter the residence.

"Morning, ma'am."

Loren stared at the sentries as she fought the urge to let her jaw drop open. Both men inclined their heads as they went. Simple courtesy was extended only now.

Well, that told her all she needed to know. Chris was gone. Even his memory was no longer rattling her chain. The last bit of tension bled away as the sun crept over the forest.

A secret smile lifted her face as she considered Rourke. She'd made it out of his bed this time. No small feat. The man appeared to have internal radar. Taking her mug with her, Loren stepped down the stairs and along the driveway.

The morning was stunning and she needed a little exercise. She wove into the forest as she marveled at the pure beauty of nature. The trees were thick. They spread their branches out in a canopy that broke the sunlight into golden rays. They rained down on her as she filled her lungs with the fresh scent of pine.

Rourke brushed against her mind. She let a rather smug grin spread across her face. There was the faint trace of male pride floating between them. Looking up, Loren noticed that she'd just about reached the top of the ridge.

She dug her feet into the ground intent on making it to the top. She'd looked up at the peak from the kitchen window for what felt like endless hours. Today, she was going to stand on it and look down at the house.

The trees thinned as she made the last few yards. Her lungs labored in the thin mountain air as Loren lifted her knees to cover the last few feet.

A solid grip yanked her out of her step instead. She landed against the solid wall of muscle and watched arms close around her like steel bands.

"Good morning, honey."

"How did you find me?"

Silence met her question. Loren shifted but Rourke didn't release her. His chest rose with a deep breath as he severed the link between their minds. The rejection made her angry as she pushed against his hold.

"You could just tell me it's none of my business, Campbell." His arms released her as Loren refused to give up her battle. She turned to look at the iron mask he'd slipped into place. The man pushed into her thoughts anytime he wanted to but refused to share anything about himself with her. Her temper rose up as Rourke stood inspecting her with suspicious eyes.

"Well, maybe you should just stay out of my head then. I told you before, I don't play stupid for anyone."

Loren rubbed her arms as her temper failed to hold off the hurt that invaded her heart. "Not even for you."

But it was a lie. Loren knew she'd play stupid for Rourke. She lifted her chin as his face turned angry. His eyes cut into hers as he very precisely pushed into her thoughts.

"I mean it, Rourke! Don't play with me."

She was so damn tempting. Rourke was mesmerized by her. Loren didn't just deal with his life, she shouldered it like a professional.

"I'm a psychic tracker, Loren. I can find anyone, dead or alive, that I have personal property from. In your case, I can link with our relationship and follow you anywhere."

Her temper completely deserted her. Instead Loren felt her heart swell with emotion. Rourke had never shared anything personal with her. He'd taken her body and soul yet never divulged his private life to her.

His hand cupped her chin as he stepped forward. "Empathy is a secondary ability, but emotions can be tricky to understand."

"Is that why I feel your thoughts sometimes?"

"Yes. I'm the only member of my family who has joined the Army outright. I command these men but I'm their operative as well."

Rourke dropped her chin as he clenched his fists with anger. He'd never felt so trapped in his entire life. "Loren, I don't exist. Can you understand that? I can't ask you to be my girlfriend, and God help me, I'm hoping you are pregnant because then I can trap you here with me."

Rourke watched her face as he spoke. His words were hard and he knew it. The best thing he could do was make her detest him. Loren had a life that she'd carved out of insurmountable odds and he didn't have the right to put her on a chain that wouldn't reach back into her world.

"I can't leave this life, Loren. My world will swallow yours without a single hesitation. It may have already cost you your life."

"I am not going to get sick." The guilt on his face made her mad. Loren felt actual rage rising in her throat. Fate had another think coming if any force in the cosmos thought it was coming between them. Love never submitted to bounds!

Her emotions zipped right across the air and into Rourke before Loren even thought to question the word love. It was simply there. There wasn't another word to use and she flatly didn't want to find a substitute. Rourke's eyebrows dipped as he tried to understand her feelings but she felt his seeking hers out in the tight bond that they'd always craved from each other.

"I will not get sick, Rourke. That's not the first time I've been coated with infected blood."

"There's one hell of a difference, Loren, and you know it."

"It hasn't convinced you to keep me at arm's length, so it can't be all that bad."

He stalked toward her and captured her body against his own. Loren laid her hands on his chest as his mouth thoroughly engaged hers in a deep kiss.

"Nothing will keep me away from you, honey, not even death."

He growled his words as Loren felt her blood begin to surge through her veins. She slipped her hands around his neck as his staff began to harden against her stomach.

"Then I guess you have a week to work on that plan."

Rourke tightened his hold as she surrendered completely to his body. No hint of struggle remained in her thoughts. Instead she gently rubbed against his body as she raised her eyes to look into his with expectation.

"What plan is that?"

"To impregnate me." Her hips rotated and rubbed the bulge of his swollen sex. "You might want to work on increasing the odds."

He released her, making her frown. Loren tried to contain her disappointment but the deep rumble of amusement from Rourke made her raise her eyes to look into his face. Desire blazed from his eyes as he opened his shirt. Her eyes dropped to the chest he revealed to her. He bent to lay the shirt open on the ground.

Rising back up, his hands made quick work of her own shirt. That garment was laid down making a larger spot. Color heated her face as she considered him wanting to make love right there. She felt terribly exposed. Loren twisted her head in both directions as she tried to assure herself that they were alone.

Rourke laughed again as he caught her chin with his hand. "I told you, honey, I don't care who watches us."

It was an arrogant statement. Primitive in the extreme but it made heat pool in her belly. Rourke intended to stake his claim on her.

"Unhook that damn bra. I hate that thing."

Loren reached for the hooks as she looked at the pants he still wore.

"Sorry, honey, I can get caught with my pants down but not off."

The statement was a reminder of the reality of his life. Loren freed her breasts as his hands found her waistband and pulled the elastic sweatpants down her legs.

She felt oddly vulnerable completely bare. The sunlight streamed down to display every last inch of her body to him. His hands lifted her off her feet as he adjusted her into position on their spread clothing.

"God, I love your breasts." His eyes were focused on the twin globes as he dipped down to suck one nipple into his mouth. Loren gasped as pleasure erupted throughout her body in response. Her skin flushed as his tongue circled the tip of the nipple even as he continued to suck. A hand gently gripped her other breast and Loren felt her passage moisten for him.

The smell of the forest struck her as intensely arousing. The faint scent of water in the ground beneath her touched some deeply rooted need to be part of nature's cycle.

His lips left her nipple and searched for the opposite one. Loren moaned as she felt the folds of her sex swell. She let her legs fall open as she suddenly needed to let those delicate folds open.

"Jesus, you smell so hot."

Rourke looked into her eyes as he drew in a deep breath. His nostrils flared slightly as Loren felt fluid sliding down the walls of her passage. His fingers gently rubbed the length of her sex as he sniffed the air again.

He wasn't an animal. Rourke clenched his teeth tightly as her scent made his body rage with need. Every time he caught her scent, primitive need roared through his brain until he was reduced to nothing but the desire to mount her.

The thick fluid from her body coated his fingers as she frantically reached for his fly. Rourke groaned as she freed his staff and wrapped her fingers around his length.

"Ah hell, Loren, I can't seem to slow down."

Rolling back, Rourke captured her hips and brought her over his body. Loren gasped with pleasure as the tip of his staff probed the opening to her passage. She let her thighs settle on either side of his body as his hand lowered her onto his. Her body welcomed the hard thrust of male flesh before he lifted her and lowered her body again.

She took the rhythm from him. Rourke groaned as she used her thighs to ride him. Her body was hot and wet as she rose and fell. He reached for her breasts as the round globes bounced with her movements. Her skin turned ruddy as climax crested over her. Rourke reached forward to rub her little bud as he bucked into her body.

Loren didn't think she'd survive. Her body was drawn too tight. It snapped in a wave of pleasure so deep it made her womb contract. She actually felt the walls of her passage clench around that hard flesh buried inside her. A stream of hot fluid shot upwards into her body making a second wave of pleasure contract around his cock.

She collapsed onto his chest. Rourke smoothed his hand over her skin, trying to absorb every last second of contact with her. Separation was stalking them like a hungry predator. Picking off their minutes together one by one. Loren had yielded everything. It should have satisfied him. Instead Rourke stared at reality and cursed.

Chapter Fourteen

A week later, Loren awoke to incoming aircraft.

The walls of the house actually shook. Loren opened her eyes as Rourke stroked her face one last time. She was draped across his bare chest. Raising her head, she looked into his eyes. Dark shadows betrayed the fact that he hadn't slept very much. Early evening light filtered through the blinds as the windows rattled violently once again.

"Here come the troops."

Her clothing landed on her bare body as Loren brought her eyes around to Rourke. His face was deadly serious as he efficiently donned his fatigues. His motions were razor-sharp.

Kicking her legs over the edge of the bed, Loren followed his example. The noise drifting up from the front of the house told her they had company and that the hourglass had run dry. She'd kept her word and failed to develop even the hint of a symptom of Tai Forest.

Their quarantine was over.

Rourke caught her against his body. His mouth captured hers in a deep kiss that lingered even after he pulled away.

"Finish dressing and come out. It's time to tie up the details."

Still struggling with her bra, Loren didn't look up 'til Rourke had left. She frowned at the empty doorframe and reached for her shirt. The man transformed from lover into Major in one second flat. The week they'd spent in bed evaporated with the morning sun.

The hallway was full of the sounds from the rotors of multiple helicopters. Loren followed the noise until she stood in the front doorframe. Technically, she was still in the house. The front drive now held three additional helicopters.

The men who stepped down from the aircraft were all wearing the green and brown fatigues. It was like she'd stepped into an action movie. Her white tee-shirt was the gleaming exception to the military dress code.

Rourke lifted his head to focus his eyes on her. The man in front of him turned to eye her as well.

Rourke was a big man. His companion was a giant. His eyes caught hers before he turned to walk toward her.

"Lavender Rain Loren?"

"Yes." God, she hated her name! Loren looked past the man for a moment as her father stepped down from one of the aircraft.

The small insignias sitting on the giant's collar said he was a Colonel-General. The highest rank a Colonel obtained before getting his first star. It was an achievement most officers never got to wear.

Letting her eyes travel over the collection of classified helicopters and armed men, Loren decided finding a man here with this rank wasn't really that surprising. Add in the word psychic and she felt a little shiver shake her spine. Top secret might be used in modern moviemaking, but this was the real thing.

That shiver left a tingle behind in her brain. Loren considered the feeling as she looked around for Rourke.

No one brushed her mind like that except for him. Instead she looked into another pair of emerald green eyes. These didn't belong to another brother. Loren found herself staring at a woman who was smaller than she was.

Coal black hair was pinned on top of her head. She was inspecting Loren with those eyes exactly like Rourke did, only it was clear she held a wealth of experience in the art.

The corners of her mouth lifted as Loren felt her releasing her hold on her mind. Rourke stepped up onto the porch to offer the woman a hug. Loren couldn't help but smile. She was half the size of her son, but it was very clear that this was the woman responsible for raising Rourke into the man that he was. She embraced her son with clear joy.

A man stepped forward and waited for his turn. He was the only one not wearing military fatigues. The tan uniform declared him to be from the local Sheriff's Department. His face told Loren that this was Rourke's father.

The men walked down the steps to join the group of military men. Loren keenly felt her civilian status as she stood on the porch uncertain about what was happening. No one offered to fill her in, either. There was a clear line separating her from the current activity.

And Rourke walked away with his men.

"I am Grace Campbell."

Loren turned and smiled at the first female she'd seen in almost a month, although Rourke's mother was certainly not in the same category as any woman that Loren knew. There was an ease that she displayed around the military precision that surrounded them. She was part of the group that Loren was excluded from.

"Grace!" Colonel Jacobs aimed his voice up to the porch, making Grace shake her head.

"We've been summoned."

"I guess we'd better fall in then."

Grace didn't agree but kept her mouth closed. Her son was being stubborn and she wanted no part of it, but emotions often unsettled the most basic of people. When it came to love, even the most practical of humans reacted with disbelief.

Grace considered Rourke a moment, and thought that her son was very much like his father. Brice Campbell had once declared that she would never outrun him and Grace decided that Loren would discover that facet of the Campbell personality...firsthand.

Everyone was loading into the aircraft. Loren followed Grace as the woman walked straight to one of the Panthers and climbed aboard. A Ranger held the rear door open for Loren, making her angry. She knew how to get into a helicopter all by herself!

She let her temper rise as the aircraft lifted off the ground. Loren embraced the heat of temper because otherwise she just might remember that Rourke had boarded a different helicopter.

The black aircraft rose above the house where she'd learned so much, before they circled around to come back around to face the compound. Two trails of smoke headed toward the house before the structure exploded into a fireball. Flames shot up into the morning air as another round of missiles were fired at it.

Loren slapped a hand over her mouth as she watched the complete destruction of every last thing that could remind her that Rourke Campbell had ever really existed.

The pilot turned the aircraft away from the fire. Loren felt her emotions drain away as the mountains gave way to the suburbs of the city limits. They touched down at a small city airport where the local Sheriff's Department took charge of putting her onto a commercial plane.

Toby didn't even accompany her on the flight back to southern California. Instead Loren stared at the letter that her son had written to her. Dr. Jasper had decided it was time for her son to expand his mind at M.I.T.

It was better that way. Loren folded the letter and tightened her resolve. She'd always known it had to end…and so it had.

Chapter Fifteen

"You know, for a man who just cheated death. You look mighty unhappy with the result."

Rourke tossed a blackened timber into a growing pile before growling at Clay.

"Shut up."

Clay laughed instead.

"Clay, stop being an ass."

Jared Campbell stepped up beside Rourke to survey the remains of the house. Thin tapers of smoke still rose from the blacken skeleton. Rourke lifted an eyebrow as he noticed that Jared had come wearing an old set of fatigues. A pair of work gloves was half tucked into the waistband.

"You plan on helping this fool?" Clay looked at the mess the fire had left and then back at his brothers. "Can't you two wait until it at least cools off completely?"

"No." Rourke went back to work. Insanity was hot on his heels and he needed the work to help outrun it. There was an empty cavern in the center of his chest that was about to kill him.

"All right, let me call in some equipment."

"My men will be here in twenty minutes with it." Jared yanked his gloves on and joined Rourke as the two men began to break down some of the remaining plumbing. Everything had to go before construction could begin on a new home.

Rourke considered the look Jared gave him. A grin lifted the corner of his mouth as Jared raised that eyebrow higher.

"You were right, it's bloody intense."

Jared laughed in a low rumble as Clay joined the labor. "What's intense?"

Rourke turned to look at his younger brother.

"You'll know when you run into that preacher's daughter."

"Let's get one thing clear me hermanos… Due to the fine example you two fools have set for me, I am never going to fall in love."

"What's the matter with love?"

Brice Campbell pulled a work glove onto his own hand as the mountain flooded with men all preparing to help out their comrade.

Rourke watched Clay roll his eyes as their father gave him the raised eyebrow of authority. Love was overwhelming. It was digging a trench through his mind as he searched for the gentle touch that Loren and he had shared only one short day ago. Love was the gut-wrenching fear that she'd be happier back in her life.

Love was Goddamn intense!

* * * * *

Fit for duty.

Such a simple phrase. Loren dragged her steps as she made her way toward the medical center lab. There was nothing familiar about the course. There should have been. An exam was routine in her high-risk profession. Blood tests a monthly event.

She suddenly felt like a stranger in the very hallways that she'd made into her home. The white tile of the hospital corridor was so plain. Loneliness wrapped around her as silence filled her ears.

Rourke Campbell had filled every second of the day.

Lifting her chin, she smiled. There were no regrets. She'd lay the memories aside and enjoy them one at a time for each night of her life.

The lab was efficient and handed over her results. Loren scanned the numbers before she felt her heart drop yet again. Negative. She was fit for duty.

She wasn't pregnant. With that simple blood test, left the last hope she had of seeing Rourke again.

"Welcome back, Loren, missed you."

"Thanks."

"Captain already has orders for you."

"That so?" Loren smiled at Cammy, the senior lab nurse, before she turned toward the locker room. Orders sounded great. Having been off duty for a month, her position had been filled on the flight schedule. It would take another couple of weeks to rotate her back in. There was a waiting list a mile long for her position on the helicopter but she would get it back.

In the meantime, Loren had feared she'd be delegated to emergency room duty. Being stuck in the hospital was near drudgery. Yup, orders sounded great! Even doing elementary school fire awareness programs would beat ER watch. That was a job they stuck the new emergency medical technicians on for them to gain experience in a place where there was someone to take up any slack they might leave.

She turned toward her locker. Loren buttoned up her uniform and adjusted her badge before making her way to the Captain's office. The new firefighter stuck on desk duty smiled at her while his face was plastered with his boredom. The office had to be staffed by fire department personnel. Otherwise they didn't have a clue how to deal with the job. The young man on duty was clearly counting the days until he was finished and could report to a firehouse.

"Loren, reporting for duty."

A yellow envelope was handed over. Loren felt a true smile lift her mouth as she broke the seal. If the orders were sealed, the assignment promised to be something worth keeping quiet.

Her face fell a second later. Loren felt her blood freeze in her veins as she tried to absorb the three lines printed on the paper.

"Loren! Get your tail into my office!"

"Yes, sir."

She walked while still trying to understand her orders.

"Who in the hell is Sheriff Brice Campbell anyway?" Captain Murray hit the top of his desk as he glared at her. "He's got one hell of a nerve stealing one of my flight medics."

Murray kicked his chair back and aimed a finger at her. "Well, you don't have to go. Just say the word and I'll call the stinking governor myself and tell him to go to hell. Damn governor thinks he can reassign you because some Washington sheriff wants a top of the line flight medic…well, he can find another one!"

Loren didn't say a word. Instead she felt her body flush with warmth. In her hand was the ticket to join Rourke…if she had the courage to take it.

"Excuse me sir, but the helo is on the roof, looking for her."

The young firefighter ducked out of the door as Captain Murray exploded.

"They can rot up there!" Murray shook his finger again. "A governor's orders are mighty hard to disobey… But you call me and I'll find a way to get you back."

"Hey, Cap, don't worry so much. I'll handle it."

Murray nodded as he mumbled about suits telling him how to run his station. Loren turned and faced the elevator doors. In front of her stood a decision too large to grasp. If Rourke couldn't admit to loving her, she couldn't hang around waiting for it. Life was too short to waste on half-living. Loren wanted it all or nothing.

She stepped out of the elevator and into the loud noise of a helicopter on the landing pad. Her body fell into step out of memory but she blinked her eyes as she took in the Panther sitting on the pad.

The pilot cut the rotor as Rourke jumped to the ground. His body was still the most amazing thing she'd ever set eyes on. Strength radiated from him, making her smile.

He stopped and stared at her. His eyes were hidden behind mirror shades as he hooked his hands into his belt. He yanked the glasses off before talking the last step between them.

"I hate that uniform on you."

He grinned at her like a boy even as his eyes returned to her badge and sharpened into slits. Loren felt her emotions surge forward. But she clamped them solidly within her. Rourke had never been a man to leave loose ends.

"I'm not pregnant."

"Would you like to be?"

Loren gasped. His voice offered a temptation so tempting, yet so unrealistic. His eyes watched hers with that razor-sharpness she knew so well. He offered his hand palm up.

"My dad is rather excited about having a real paramedic on duty. Benton is so remote, no one ever wants the job. But we've got the need for a modern department." He grinned and offered his hand closer. "But I've got one condition."

"That would be?"

"You have to make an honest man of me."

"Are you asking me to marry you?" Loren whispered the words. Her hope grew with each one that left her lips. Rourke's face fell into a solid mask as he reached forward and caught her chin.

"I'm asking you to get on that helo and follow me home. Leave a posting you worked your butt off for and join a small-town fire department. Move into my brother's house because mine burned to the ground." His fingers tightened on her jaw as his voice dipped into a low growl. "I'm asking you to let me spend the rest of my life loving you. To take a chance on marriage with a man who is demanding and stubborn but who loves you more then he can say."

Tears burned her eyes. Loren tried to force even a single word out of her throat, instead she simply smiled.

Joy radiated through her body chasing any doubt still clinging to her memories away.

Life wasn't fair and love wasn't predictable. It struck without warning. Transforming lives and merging souls.

"Show me the way to the preacher…solider man."

Enjoy this excerpt from
Dream Shadow
Dream
© Copyright Mary Wine 2004

The sound rain made as it fell was perfect. Grace let the corners of her mouth drop into a frown as a sharp whistle shattered it. Considering the thunderclouds above her she shut her eyes and ears to any more interruptions. Tipping her head back, she smiled as the icy droplets slid across her cheeks.

Freedom. Plain, simple and found right here where the forests of Washington began.

"Grace."

It was amazing the way Major Jason Jacobs could turn her name into a low growl of pure disgruntlement. Aiming her eyes into the night, Grace considered the forest with a longing that bordered on need.

"There's no need for a hotel, Major." Grace considered the forest again. "Let's camp."

"I heard it's been raining for two straight weeks, we'll be drowning in mud." The frustration in the Major's voice was rapidly turning into indignant male pride. The problem with having conversations with any Officer was you never knew just when they he would take an opinion as a slight to his authority. But male pride could often be amusing to watch.

"I'd prefer to camp."

"*Grace…*"

Grace raised her shoulder slightly in a shrug as she looked back at the freedom she was going to be denied. Turning on her heel she fell into step with the rest of her escort. The men of Jacobs' Unit stood impatiently waiting for her to embrace being shoved into a hotel room neatly stored away.

Tonight the night was alive, and that life came sailing straight at her. The abundance of it prevented any true understanding of just what it was. Spinning on her heel, Grace faced it head-on. Nothing but silence greeted her, yet the ringing echo was almost deafening.

"What is it?"

Snapping her head about, she regarded Jacobs. With his head slightly tilted in her direction, he stood patiently waiting for her to finish. Maybe the man was traditional enough to prefer a bed to the forest floor, but he had never forced her to abandon any vision before she captured it completely.

Whatever floated on the wind, the scent of it somehow made the forest even more enticing. Pulling the fragments of emotion into her mind, Grace slowly attempted to force them into focus.

The vision eluded her grasp, leaving behind an increasing hunger to track it down. Exactly why her curiosity was involved was a mystery. Caring about an assignment was trouble. Any emotional involvement would become the key to misery. Shaking her head in frustration, Grace turned back to Jacobs' Unit.

Too bad, for a moment life had almost begun to get interesting.

Maybe it was simple frustration that drove Grace to seek out the vision again. Maybe it was pure distaste for the stale confines of her motel room. Whatever the cause, Grace sat poised on her knees while she tried to assemble the bits of feeling she held into a recognizable picture.

Major Jacobs could get his six hours of sleep. Grace might know better than to care about a mission but she'd already committed the sin of curiosity. Letting that small scrap of emotion get into her head was going to keep any type of sleep well and truly separated from her tonight.

There was too much emotional bleed-out from the community. Anger, fear, hope and half a dozen other feelings were floating through the night. Grace couldn't just feel it; she was almost drowning in it.

Grace forced her mind into sharp control. She needed to focus to keep it all from blurring. This time, the connection with her mind was clear. The vision blossomed into full color commanding her complete attention.

Grace could see every single hair on her target's head. The emotion of curiosity crumbled away and left Grace with the unmistakable feeling of need. Her vision wasn't a target any longer. It became a child and Grace could see her as clear as day. The night was literally singing. Grace was impatient to become a part of the harmony.

Holding the vision at bay, Grace turned towards the room's door. Her feet faltered as she caught the feeling of one of the Rangers. There was always a perimeter sentry posted at night.

Slipping along side the window, she pulled the curtain away a bare inch to catch sight of the man. It wasn't that she held any true dislike for Clark, but the man thought she was a witch. He wasn't alone in that. Half the men that made up Jacobs' Unit thought she was some sort of devil's handmaiden.

Tonight, the ugly label stirred her temper. She didn't want to share the pure innocence of her vision with men that wanted to condemn her as a heathen. She wanted to touch this child, immerse herself in the uncomplicated bliss of early childhood.

The Unit could be damned. Grace wasn't in the mood to be judged and she wasn't going to wait for daybreak.

* * * * *

So, they were here.

More exactly, she was here. Brice continued to observe the three helicopters that currently sat on the asphalt in front of what served as the Benton County Airport. It was painfully easy to pick out the woman amidst the unit of Army Rangers. Even at his current distance, her slight build was obvious compared with that of her companions.

Brice sunk back into the seat of his patrol jeep. The men left on duty were armed to deadly precision, including night-vision goggles. It had taken him almost two days, along with every favor that a living soul owed him on this planet to get this bunch into Benton County.

There was no need to get started on the wrong foot. The instructions he had been given were painfully clear. The airfield was to be cleared.

It was, but there was no way that he was going to sit by waiting for this group to run him like a dog on a leash. This was his county; he just hoped he was making the right decision.

Turning the ignition over, he pulled the jeep back on to the road. There was nothing right about this whole thing. Three years into his first term as Sheriff, Brice had seen a lot of things cross his path. Child abduction just wasn't something that he ever thought to see in front of him. A man could fail to solve a burglary, maybe even a murder, but how could you fail to find someone's little girl?

Brice closed his eyes for a moment. He was really reaching this time. When it got out he was bringing in a psychic, it could very well cost him his re-election next year. Benton was a small community; nothing stayed a secret for long. By the end of next week rumors, if not the whole story, would be all over the county. If this Unit failed to turn up Paige Heeley, Brice could more than likely kiss his office goodbye.

If this psychic bloodhound turned up his missing little girl, Brice didn't give a damn about his office. Paige was just four years old and Brice would gladly take the heat once the family was reunited.

The entire idea of a psychic being helpful still stuck in the back of his throat. Swallowing that concept was going to require some hard evidence.

This one might be different. Whatever his own feelings about the paranormal aside, he was left with one hard fact. The United States Army didn't tend to waste its time.

For some reason, this woman was part of a Ranger Unit. Brice was about to wager a great deal on her being half as good as the rumors he'd heard about her.

Now if they just managed to turn something up. Brice had every able-bodied man out searching and they hadn't turned up so much as a hair ribbon. After two weeks, any hope of recovering the child alive was almost gone.

Well, Brice wasn't ready to give her up to the mountains. Paige Heeley was out there and maybe, just maybe, he had found the means to finding her.

About the author:

I write to reassure myself that reality really is survivable. Between traffic jams and children's sporting schedules, there is romance lurking for anyone with the imagination to find it.

I spend my days making corsets and petticoats as a historical costumer. If you send me an invitation marked formal dress, you'd better give a date or I just might show up wearing my bustle.

I love to read a good romance and with the completion of my first novel, I've discovered I am addicted to writing these stories as well.

Dream big or you might never get beyond your front yard.

I love to hear what you think of my writing: Talk2MaryWine@hotmail.com.

Mary welcomes mail from readers. You can write to her c/o Ellora's Cave Publishing at 1056 Home Avenue, Akron OH 44310-3502.

Why an electronic book?

We live in the Information Age—an exciting time in the history of human civilization in which technology rules supreme and continues to progress in leaps and bounds every minute of every hour of every day. For a multitude of reasons, more and more avid literary fans are opting to purchase e-books instead of paperbacks. The question to those not yet initiated to the world of electronic reading is simply: *why?*

1. *Price.* An electronic title at Ellora's Cave Publishing and Cerridwen Press runs anywhere from 40-75% less than the cover price of the <u>exact same title</u> in paperback format. Why? Cold mathematics. It is less expensive to publish an e-book than it is to publish a paperback, so the savings are passed along to the consumer.

2. *Space.* Running out of room to house your paperback books? That is one worry you will never have with electronic novels. For a low one-time cost, you can purchase a handheld computer designed specifically for e-reading purposes. Many e-readers are larger than the average handheld, giving you plenty of screen room. Better yet, hundreds of titles can be stored within your new library—a single microchip. (Please note that Ellora's Cave and Cerridwen Press does not endorse any specific brands. You can check our website at www.ellorascave.com or

www.cerridwenpress.com for customer recommendations we make available to new consumers.)

3. *Mobility.* Because your new library now consists of only a microchip, your entire cache of books can be taken with you wherever you go.

4. *Personal preferences are accounted for.* Are the words you are currently reading too small? Too large? Too...**ANNOYING**? Paperback books cannot be modified according to personal preferences, but e-books can.

5. *Instant gratification.* Is it the middle of the night and all the bookstores are closed? Are you tired of waiting days—sometimes weeks—for online and offline bookstores to ship the novels you bought? Ellora's Cave Publishing sells instantaneous downloads 24 hours a day, 7 days a week, 365 days a year. Our e-book delivery system is 100% automated, meaning your order is filled as soon as you pay for it.

Those are a few of the top reasons why electronic novels are displacing paperbacks for many an avid reader. As always, Ellora's Cave and Cerridwen Press welcomes your questions and comments. We invite you to email us at service@ellorascave.com, service@cerridwenpress.com or write to us directly at: 1056 Home Ave. Akron OH 44310-3502.

Monday
1
Work
2
Work
3
Work
Work
Work
8
Work
9
Work
10
Work
11
Work
12
Work
15
Work
16
Work
17
Work
18
Work
19
22
Work
23
Work
24
Work
25
Work
26

THE
ELLORA'S CAVE
LIBRARY

Stay up to date with Ellora's Cave Titles
in Print with our Quarterly Catalog.